CRYSTAL LAKE GIFTS

A Novel

BOOK 2 - CRYSTAL LAKE SERIES

Susan W. Green

ISBN: Paperback 979-8-9853114-2-6
ISBN: Ebook 979-8-9853114-3-3

Michele Chynoweth, Editor
Design and publishing assistance by The Happy Self-Publisher.

DEDICATION

I've always loved the phrase, "It takes a village to get things done," and I agree. While writing can be a solitary effort, my husband and family support my journey and patiently listen to me talk about fictional characters, debate scenes, locations, and names.

A huge thank you to Glenda, who proofread countless revisions, and to my advanced readers. Also, thanks to my special Mainer, Melissa, for sharing deep knowledge of her home state.

It absolutely took a village to get this book into the hands of readers. Enjoy Crystal Lake Gifts.

CHAPTER ONE

"My dream is finally coming true…I can't believe this is happening!" Trish Cavanaugh tried not to yell at the top of her lungs as she stepped into the empty retail space on Main Street, but she couldn't help herself. "I'm so excited. I can hardly wait for the grand opening of the expanded store!" Suddenly, Trish realized she was standing in front of a large picture window overlooking Main Street, talking out loud to herself. She hoped no one passing by had seen her. They would think she was crazy.

If anyone had noticed the person standing on the other side of the picture window, they would have seen a petite woman in her early thirties with long blonde hair, large blue eyes, and a bright smile. They would also have noticed she looked well put together, with expensive clothing and accessories. Yet, Trish had a way of pulling together outfits from the sales rack at local department stores and consignment shops that gave the impression she had purchased them at high-end designer shops.

Looking at the stunning woman, you would probably laugh if you knew her first choice of transportation, weather permitting, was a bright red Triumph motorcycle. It always surprised people to see Trish put on her riding gear, pull her long hair back into a tight ponytail, push it under a bright pink helmet, slip on black leather boots, and straddle the bike.

Trish often said the bike was her one guilty pleasure.

The space Trish was standing in was the only empty building on Main Street in Lewisville, Maine. The old brick buildings had been well maintained over the years, and with the downtown renovations the city had sponsored several years ago, the increased foot traffic on Main Street made these storefronts a well-sought-after retail space.

When a real estate agent approached Trish to let her know the building adjoining her store was going up for sale, she didn't waste any time signing the form to take it off the market. It was the perfect opportunity to expand her gift shop, Crystal Lake Gifts.

It was destiny telling her it was the right thing to do—at least, that's what Trish convinced herself to believe. It was the perfect set-up. A connecting door was already between her existing store and the new space. The door had never been unlocked since Trish bought her gift shop five years ago… until now.

While Trish had crunched the numbers with her accountant several times, the reality of what she had done now caused her stomach to do summersaults. It wasn't only the added mortgage payments but also the renovations, additional furniture, display cases, and merchandise expenses.

The bottom line was a staggering number. She was confident she could make it work and double the size of her business. She would become a successful businesswoman and realize her dream, but only if she stayed focused and did not get sidetracked along the way.

After three weeks of haggling over the purchase price, Trish had signed the mortgage papers earlier in the day.

She hoped her grandmother, Nana, would be proud of her. Nana was a special person in Trish's childhood and college years and helped set her on the road to success. As Trish thought about how she got to where she is today, she couldn't help but dredge up childhood memories.

Trish's parents had met in high school. They attended the same college, where they both majored in finance. Once they got their CPAs, they planned to open their own accounting firm. But at the end of their sophomore year of college, her mother discovered she was pregnant with Trish, and their plans were thrown into chaos. The couple had to quit school for several years. They got low-paying jobs and prepared to be parents.

Her parents had worked day and night for several years until they finally returned to college. Once they graduated and obtained their CPA licenses, the couple put all their effort into growing their firm and turning it into a lucrative business. But money remained tight.

Trish's father never seemed happy. Instead, he was always chasing an intangible dream. Her father took out several loans for fancy cars and a boat, thinking that would make him happy. But, eventually, working sixty-hour weeks, raising a child, and trying to pay off their massive debt took its toll on the marriage and the business.

One argument led to another. Soon, the couple was constantly bickering, and both were unhappy. Trish could hear them arguing when she lay in bed at night, covering her ears to avoid the drama.

When a rival CPA firm opened in the same town, clients started to leave the small family company, and finally, her father gave up. He sold the CPA firm without discussing it with her mom.

Trish's last memory of her father was the night before he left for good. Her parents intensely argued about the firm's sale, the lack of discussion about the deal, and the debt piling up. They were oblivious that their young daughter stood in the doorway with tears streaming down her cheeks.

The following day, her mother found a note from her father on the kitchen counter that said he was a failure and couldn't take it anymore. He was leaving behind the money in their savings account, but was keeping the cash from the firm's sale to start over elsewhere. He didn't want any contact with them. He was basically running away and leaving Trish and her mother to start over alone.

Trish never saw her father again.

Several months later, a Maine State Police officer showed up at their door and said her father had been killed in a car accident. Since they were still legally married, it fell to her mother to take care of the funeral and clean up the financial mess her father had left. A few days after the small funeral, an out-of-state attorney contacted her mom to say his client had left a will, but over the last several months of his life, he'd withdrawn most of the money and lost it gambling at a casino in Connecticut.

After that, her mom went in and out of various stages of depression. Finally, Trish's maternal grandmother moved in with them to help care for Trish and her mom.

Trish's grandmother, Nana, was a loving and caring person, and Trish flourished under her care. Nana always told Trish she could be whatever she wanted to be and accomplish anything if she tried hard enough. Trish had promised Nana she would study hard, own her own company, and be a successful businesswoman when she grew up. As a result, Trish never wanted to depend on another person for her happiness or financial security.

Right after Trish graduated from high school, her mother passed away. The doctor said it was from an undiagnosed heart defect, but Trish knew her mom died of a crushed spirit and a broken heart.

The estate was left to Trish, along with a small amount of life insurance she could access on her twenty-fifth birthday and a few family heirlooms from Nana, who passed away a year later. Trish used those funds to purchase her first store, located at 300 Main Street, which she named Crystal Lake Gifts. The store became a success and was now one of the anchor stores on Main Street.

The pinging of a text message brought her back to reality. The text let her know the electric service had been transferred into her name. One more item she could check off her long list of things to do.

Trish walked around the space, stopping in the middle of the room. She closed her eyes to try and imagine how it would look once the renovations were done. Trish saw custom cabinets along the wall connecting the two shops and gleaming glass from antique display cases. She quickly decided the cases she had in storage would be placed next to the large picture windows running along the front of the building. The beveled glass would make everything inside the cases sparkle and shimmer on sunny days, and the addition of subtle lighting from new sconces and overhead lights would keep the entire space well-lit.

Opening her eyes, Trish slowly walked over to the far wall where she hoped to put the new upscale clothing line she had been dying to launch. The extra space allowed an attractive display of clothing, shoes, and accessories. In addition, the nook area in the corner was the perfect location for two new fitting rooms.

That still left the wall at the far end of the new space. There was more than enough room for a series of cabinets and shelves. *Perfect,* Trish said to herself since she also had a plan to fill those shelves.

While waiting for the real estate deal to close, Trish took a risk and hired an architect to draw up plans to tentatively include space for another merchant. Trish was quite sure Sarah Jennings would be the perfect tenant.

Now that the deal had been signed, she planned to speak to Sarah, who headed up the local artisans' cooperative, to see if she'd be interested in leasing space in the expanded store. The organization would finally have a retail space to sell its gorgeous handmade items.

Still in thought, Trish was startled when she heard the bell clanging over the door in her existing space and turned to hurry back to her shop. As she opened the antique wooden door between the two areas, she was thrilled to see her best friends, Cassidy Taylor Burnett and Amanda Blake.

Trish stayed in the empty room and called her friends to join her. "I'm in here!"

The two women walked into the vacant space, headed straight toward Trish, and engulfed her in a big hug.

Cassidy turned around to look at the large room. "I can't wait to see what you do with this old shop. It's a shame it was only used for storage for several years and hasn't been renovated in decades. I bet there will be some challenges along the way, but I know you'll turn it into a great retail space."

Amanda stepped back from the group hug and looked over at Trish, "Have you spoken to Sarah yet? Now that the junk has been cleared out, it looks like there's enough room for everything you wanted to do in the new space and options for the local artisans."

"No, I haven't had the chance to call her yet. I didn't want to get Sarah's hopes up until the deal was officially done. Unfortunately, the former owner's attorney was difficult to deal with, and things dragged on for a few extra weeks. I was certain they didn't have another offer for the space, so I threatened to walk away from the deal. Finally, the attorney agreed to my terms. We signed the final paperwork this morning at ten o'clock."

Leading her friends back into her existing shop, Trish walked over to the front door, twisted the sign from open to closed, and started turning off the lights. "Let's go celebrate at The Perk," Trish announced.

The women headed out the door and walked across the street. Fortunately for three coffee lovers, The Perk, the best coffee place in town, was across the street from Crystal Lake Gifts. It was a great place to hear the latest gossip and to catch up on the latest trials, triumphs, and matters of the heart.

CHAPTER TWO

Several years ago, Sarah Jennings had pulled together the local art and crafting community and formed a small co-op with help from the Lakeview Town Council. Sarah was an artist in her own right, yet she also had a savvy sense for business.

Standing tall at five-feet eight-inches, she had long chestnut brown hair, typically braided, falling halfway down her back. But her emerald-green eyes and long eyelashes were her best qualities. People might not always remember her name, but they always remembered those gorgeous eyes.

The Lakeview Artisans' Cooperative Enterprise, better known as LACE, started selling items at the local farmers market and quickly became one of the market's main draws. The Lakeview Farmers Market on Main Street was a favorite not only for the residents of Lakeview but also for the influx of out-of-town guests during the summer tourist season. Unfortunately, the market was only open on Fridays and Saturdays from April through September.

Sarah had been looking for a permanent retail space for the artisans to set up shop, allowing the members to have a brick-and-mortar, year-round location. Her personal big break came when Cassidy Taylor Burnett, owner of Crystal Lake Inn, started selling Sarah's merchandise at the popular lakeside inn. The items went beyond the typical keychains and postcards, and featured handpainted aprons, mugs, placemats, and tee shirts.

Another popular item was the hand-painted picnic hampers the inn used to pack lunches their guests could order from the kitchen at the inn. The merchandise was so popular Sarah had to pull in other LACE members to keep up with the demand.

Walking down Main Street, Sarah noticed the "For Sale" sign no longer hung in the front window of the old shop next to Crystal Lake Gifts. She had entertained the possibility of buying the shop, but several challenges were in the way. For one, LACE's finances fluctuated seasonally, and their accountant warned against such a major purchase. Two, the members of the organization were split about the commitment. That put the decision on hold. Now, seeing the "For Sale" sign missing from the window, she sadly realized the opportunity to open a retail shop at one of the best locations on Main Street had been lost.

Sarah continued to stand in front of the window and lament what was lost. But being a "glass-half-full" person, she decided staring into the window wouldn't solve anything.

The wonderful aroma of freshly brewed coffee caught her attention. Her nose told her it was time to grab a coffee from The Perk. Sarah headed to the coffee shop across the street.

As she waited at the red light for the "Walk" indicator to flash, Sarah noticed the City of Lakeview maintenance crew had been busy since the last time she was downtown. The crew had placed large hanging baskets on the light poles on several blocks of Main Street and had other baskets sitting on the ground in boxes, waiting to be hung.

Sarah decided to take a closer look at the crew's work. She turned to her right and walked further up Main Street, stopping in front of one of the baskets waiting to be hung. As she looked closer, she saw a rainbow of colors erupting from the baskets—begonias in yellow, red, and purple sat next to petunias in bright pink and deep violet with long strands of green ivy flowing over the edges. In a few weeks, the effect of the rainbow of colors would turn Main Street into a floral wonderland. The overall impact of the colors and the fresh flowers would be stunning.

Finally, the "Walk" light indicated it was safe to cross the street. Sarah picked up her pace and headed to The Perk.

Stepping inside the coffee shop, she took a deep breath and smiled. The aroma of strong coffee mixed with sweets from the bakery counter made her stomach rumble, and the color scheme of subtle blues and peaches created a calming and inviting effect, precisely what she needed.

Walking up to the counter, Sarah ordered a large Dalgona, a dark, rich coffee drink that had been whipped for several minutes. It was a piece of artistic expertise and culinary delight. Sarah was always fascinated as she watched the barista make her drink. They started by adding dark-ground instant coffee granules, hot water, and sugar. Next, an electric mixer formed stiff peaks in the mahogany brown mixture, and it was topped off with a pile of creamy whipped cream, freshly shaved chocolate, and caramel bits.

The barista placed the large white ceramic cup on a rectangular tray, added a freshly baked scone sprinkled with granulated sugar, and handed the tray to Sarah. She was momentarily lost in anticipation of the sugar high she'd quickly get. Someone calling her name brought her back to reality.

Looking around for who was calling her, Sarah spotted the trio of friends sitting in their usual spot in the far corner. She waved and indicated she'd join them in a minute.

After paying for her scrumptious treat, she picked up the tray and cautiously weaved her way around tables and other guests, taking great care not to spill even one drop of her Dalgona.

When Sarah placed her tray on the table, the trio of friends stared at the frothy creation.

"Don't even think about touching my Dalgona. I only get one of these treats occasionally and plan to savor every last drop of liquid in this cup," Sarah teased. "Of course, the scone is also off-limits. On the other hand, it's nice to see the three of you, but it's a bit unusual to see you away from work on a weekday in the middle of the afternoon."

Sarah looked around the table. She could tell by the grins on her friends' faces something was up, and she planned to find out what was happening. "What's up?"

There was silence for another moment, but it was clear Trish was getting ready to burst. When she opened her mouth, the words quickly rushed out. "I bought the empty store next to Crystal Lake Gifts, and I want you to open a retail space for LACE in my expanded shop. I'm aware you considered opening a retail space there, but the numbers didn't work for your group. I think you can swing it, and we can both make a comfortable profit if you rent from me. What do you think?"

"I…umm…well…umm…" Sarah closed her mouth so she'd stop mumbling. She was caught off-guard by the offer and needed a minute to gather her thoughts. "Give me a minute to think," she said.

There was silence at the table while Sarah considered the pros and cons of Trish's offer.

Without meaning to be so loud, Sarah shouted "YES!" which drew questioning looks from several other patrons. "Yes, I would love to rent from Crystal Lake Gifts. I'll need to bring the recommendation before the LACE board, and as luck would have it, we have a meeting later today. I'm positive the vote will be yes, and it should be unanimous. I can't thank you enough, Trish. We were close to opening a retail space but never found the right deal. Renting from you will make the journey so much easier for us. You're our hero." Sarah leaned over and gave Trish a big hug.

Trish raised her mug, "Here's to great friends and a new opportunity for the local artisans. Cheers." The four women clinked their mugs together and enjoyed their coffee break while planning the new shop.

CHAPTER THREE

Several days later, Trish was in the loft above her shop on Main Street, where she'd lived since the store opened six years ago. It was convenient to live upstairs, and she couldn't complain about having a coffee shop across the street. Over time, she'd renovated the space into a comfortable apartment.

Since the structure's front façade had large windows running along the entire building, her loft had benefited from plenty of natural light. The walls were brick, and the ceiling was open with exposed ventilation pipes painted black. Ceiling lights hung from long black poles, and the inside window casings were also black, which softened the bright white kitchen cabinets and countertops. In addition, the original hardwood floors had been saved by a talented local tradesman who specialized in salvaging old floors. As a result, the oak floors now gleamed in the sunlight.

Trish loved the loft space, but with the upcoming expansion of Crystal Lake Gifts, she needed to use it for offices and meeting space. While she had mixed feelings about moving, she was fortunate her best friend, Cassidy, had insisted Trish move into one of the suites at Crystal Lake Inn until she was ready to buy a house or rent an apartment.

Homes near the lake were costly, and the decision to jump into a long-term mortgage wasn't one Trish planned to take lightly.

She was blessed to have such wonderful friends in her life. Staying at the inn also allowed her to keep in touch with Cassidy and Amanda and join them for the famous Crystal Lake Inn Sunday Brunch. No one made a better seafood casserole or lobster benedict than the inn's chef, Peter.

While packing the last moving boxes, Trish came across one of her favorite photo albums. She sat down on the worn burgundy leather sofa, curled her legs underneath her, and opened the cover. For the next hour, memories flooded Trish's mind. Most of them included at least one of her best friends.

Trish, Cassidy, and Amanda had met at college and were inseparable. The album contained many good memories and some painful ones. As Trish continued to browse, she stopped to recall events the women had experienced over the years.

She looked through college graduation pictures, which brought back bad memories of Cassidy's first true love, Ben, calling off their engagement the week before their senior finals. Cassidy was crushed, and it took her a long time to trust her judgment or make big decisions easily again.

Cassidy was a classic beauty with long light brown hair, doe-like brown eyes, and a smile for everyone. More than one person asked her if she was related to Jennifer Love Hewitt, which made her laugh. She failed to see her own good looks and charm.

Fast-forward, Cassidy found the B&B she'd always wanted to own. Trish recalled how shocked she had been when Cassidy showed her the crumbling old inn, but she quickly saw the fantastic lake views from every window. Cassidy's vision became a reality with lots of hard work and determination. Now, six years later, Cassidy's business was an enormous success.

Over the years, Cassidy added a larger dining room, additional guest rooms, a wrap-around porch, and professional landscaping. The inn was surrounded by gorgeous gardens, well-lit walkways, and benches nestled along the lake so guests could sit and enjoy the view. The inn had become a repeat favorite for many guests who booked yearly.

On the heels of that win, Cassidy found her greatest love, her husband, Jack Burnett, a successful spy novelist from New York City. Trying to get over a terrible case of writer's block, Jack stayed at the inn but kept his identity hidden. Through a series of misunderstandings and humorous incidents, the two finally got together and found true love. Trish recalled their wedding last fall, which was absolutely gorgeous.

And speaking of gorgeous, Jack fell into the same category. He was tall, with dark hair, and had the most beautiful baby-blue eyes. When Cassidy and Jack stood together at the altar, they made a striking couple, but their down-to-earth personalities kept them grounded.

Continuing to turn pages in the album, Trish came across a picture from last year's hospital fundraiser gala showing her and her friends in beautiful evening gowns. As she looked closer at the picture, it was clear Amanda and the chef from Crystal Lake Inn, Peter Cooper, also had a budding romance that had recently turned into full bloom. The couple was now living together and helping Cassidy run the inn.

Trish thought how fortunate the inn was to have Peter as the chef. He was classically trained but preferred the small-town feel of Lakeview. His meals were an experience of culinary delight, and it didn't hurt he was handsome with sea-blue eyes, wavy blond hair, and a fantastic tan he sported most of the year from being on his sailboat, which was his pride and joy.

Peter and Amanda were well-matched physically. She was a striking woman who stood at five-feet-eight inches tall, with sun-streaked light brown hair, hazel eyes, and always perfectly manicured nails. She came from an affluent New York City family, and her father had expected her to remain in their family business and live in the city. But corporate life wasn't her thing, so she packed up the contents of her fancy condominium and came to Lakeview.

After being at loose ends for a while, Cassidy had been a bit surprised when Amanda asked to work for the inn full-time, but now, several years later, she was running the day-to-day operations and loving every minute of it. When Cassidy and Jack moved to a cottage down the street from the inn, Amanda and Peter moved into the inn's owner's suite.

Meanwhile, Cassidy and Jack loved the little cottage. It had big picture windows that overlooked the lake, and the loft on the second floor was the perfect place for Jack to write. In addition, the five-minute walk to the inn allowed Cassidy to be there quickly when needed while still providing some privacy for her and Jack, especially when they were first married.

It seemed everyone's life was getting settled. *Except for mine*, Trish thought.

For Trish, her father's demise and her mother's broken spirit all pushed her to be successful. Failure was never an option. She was typically risk-averse and played it safe both professionally and personally, but the expansion of her business was a risk she was willing to take.

Of course, Trish dated occasionally, but if a relationship seemed to be moving in a more serious direction, she got scared and found a reason to end things. Friends were always trying to fix her up, but over time, they finally realized Trish protected her heart as closely as she protected her business, and they stopped being so pushy about it.

Trish focused on fulfilling her dream of owning and growing a successful business. Deciding to expand her shop didn't come easy, but she knew it was the right time to take the plunge. It was also what kept her up at night. Even though Nana had been gone for several years, Trish couldn't let her grandmother, or herself, down. She had to be a successful businesswoman. *Nothing else really matters, right?*

CHAPTER FOUR

Several weeks later, arriving in the newly renovated retail space, Trish couldn't help but smile. *Finally!* It was everything she had hoped it would be, yet it was even more thrilling than she dreamed. When the architect and designer first met with her and outlined their plans, they pointed out some potential challenges of renovating a hundred-year-old building. Trish had worried the space wouldn't be what she had envisioned. But, boy, was she wrong.

Repeating the steps she took the day she signed the deed, Trish walked around the space again and stopped in the middle of the room. Only this time, she didn't need to imagine what it would look like in the future—now she could see the outcome of the completed renovations, and it took her breath away.

She saw custom cabinets along the far walls where the items from LACE would be shown to their best advantage. Gleaming glass from the antique cases along the front windows would catch her customers' attention. In addition, the electrician had installed new wall sconces and a series of overhead lighting. So now, all areas of the retail space were bright and inviting.

The expanded retail space was set up with racks and shelves to hold the new clothing line. Trish was as excited about launching her new clothing line as she was about the artisans' handmade items.

Finally, she walked across the store and looked into the new fitting rooms. She intentionally designed larger-than-average fitting rooms and added three-sided mirrors and flattering lighting. The walls were painted a light baby blue, which helped to create a calming space. As an added touch, she included a soft, comfortable chair and a small table for purses and personal items. As a result, trying on clothes in these rooms would be enjoyable, unlike how they were in most fitting rooms. Soft music from the new overhead speakers wrapped everything in an inviting yet peaceful cocoon.

It was perfect!

A few days ago, a local moving company had moved all her furniture to a storage unit, and yesterday, Jack and Peter moved the last of her personal boxes to the inn. Tonight, Trish would get settled into her suite at the inn, and tomorrow, a large crew of helpers and employees would converge on the store to unpack boxes and stock shelves. Trish had decided to close Crystal Lake Gifts for a few days to repaint the walls, rearrange the existing furniture and display racks, and thoroughly clean the entire store. She wanted everything to be fresh, tidy, and welcoming for their Grand Opening on Monday morning.

Taking a final look around, Trish was satisfied everything was ready for the crew to start unpacking and decorating the next morning. She returned to the checkout counter, grabbed her purse and box of memorabilia, and headed down the hallway to the backdoor, where her car was parked behind the store.

Trish couldn't wait until Monday morning to unlock the doors and enter the expanded retail space. This was the next step in her career journey, and her excitement was mounting with each passing day.

It was the end of an era for Trish, but it was also the beginning of her new expanded store, a retail space for LACE, and her move to the inn. Life certainly had a way of putting twists and turns into one's path, but these were positive, and Trish was ready to make the most of the opportunities placed before her.

Nana, I'm going to make you proud.

CHAPTER FIVE

"Honestly, Peter. I can't eat another bite." Trish ate the last morsel of food on her plate.

"The seafood quiche was amazing. I've only been here a week, and I think I've already gained a few pounds. If I stay at the inn for very long, I'll have to buy a new wardrobe. But the inn is so lucky to have you as their chef. Oh, what the heck. I can't help but take full advantage of your delicious meals while I'm here."

Peter walked over to Trish's table and refilled her coffee cup. "Thank you for the compliments. I love a person who enjoys my food, and I'm happy you're staying with us for the foreseeable future. I know it makes Amanda and Cassidy incredibly happy, and anything that makes Amanda happy makes me happy."

Trish looked up at Peter. "Spoken like a man in love," she whispered, stirring sugar and cream into her coffee.

Looking around the room, Trish never failed to notice the beauty of the décor. The mahogany tables, white tablecloths, and the gorgeous view of Crystal Lake could be seen from every window along the front of the inn. The water shimmered from the bright morning sun, and the reflection bounced off the crystal glasses sitting on the side buffet.

Trish was about to ask Peter if he had seen Cassidy yet that morning when she heard laughter coming from the other side of the door connecting the dining room to the kitchen.

A moment later, Cassidy and Amanda walked into the dining room. They each grabbed a cup of coffee and headed to Trish's table.

You couldn't help but notice the two women, each striking in her own way. Amanda was several inches taller than Cassidy, and both had long brown hair, but Amanda's was sun-streaked and straighter. Since they were working at the inn today, they both wore navy blue slacks and light blue shirts with the inn's logo on the front.

Cassidy stopped and straightened the flower arrangement on the end of the sideboard. She leaned closer to the flowers to smell the wonderful fragrance of the purple crocuses, freshly cut from the inn's garden.

"Good morning, everyone. It's a beautiful spring day and I can't wait to dig into Peter's seafood quiche." Cassidy walked to the buffet table and filled her plate before sitting down.

Amanda walked over to chat with guests at the table by the front window before filling her plate and joining her friends. Peter brought over a pot of coffee, filled their cups, and sat down to join them.

"I can't wait to get to the shop this morning." Trish sipped her coffee. "We still have a few last-minute items to complete before opening the doors. And Peter, the buffet you provided last night to thank all the workers was beyond delicious. When everyone left for the evening, they were exhausted and stuffed. Thanks again to you three for everything you've done to help prepare the shop for the Grand Opening." She looked around the table and thought about how fortunate she was to have such wonderful friends. *Yes, I am incredibly blessed.*

Amanda crossed her arms with a pretend pout. "I wish Cassidy and I could be there when you open this morning, but we have a full house at the inn this week and need to stay put. If it gets too hectic, give us a call. One of us can run over to help you this afternoon once we get the rooms ready for the new guests. What time are you meeting Sarah at the shop?"

Trish looked at her watch. "We agreed to meet at nine o'clock. That gives us an hour to make last-minute changes and set out the trolly with the coffee service we planned as a special treat for our Grand Opening. I guess I better get going. As much as I'd love to sit here and drink coffee with you lovely ladies all morning, some of us have work to do."

Trish headed toward the lobby but stopped a few steps from the table and turned around, tears welling in her eyes to express what was in her heart. "Again, I can't thank you enough for your help over the past few weeks. Sometimes, I don't know what I did to deserve such wonderful friends. I'd better run if I don't want to be late. I'll give you an update tonight at dinner. You're the best friends anyone could ever hope to have. I love each one of you dearly."

"We love you too, good luck!" they said in unison.

As Trish walked out the front door and down the path to the parking area, she stopped to look back at the inn. She loved the large front porch where Cassidy served refreshments for her guests before dinner. Now that the weather was warmer, the landscaping and flower gardens would soon erupt with color, adding even more charm to the inn.

Before getting in her car, Trish looked at the calm surface of the lake and the sun reflecting off it like diamonds. It reminded her how fortunate they were to live surrounded by lakes and protected farmlands, all within an hour of Acadia National Park, the famous Cadillac Mountains, and all this region of Maine offered. Why would anyone want to live anywhere else?

A chuckle rose from her throat at her last statement as she was reminded of the freezing winter nights and the sixty inches of snowfall that fell annually. Maine wasn't for everyone, but for her, it was perfect.

Trish pulled into her usual parking spot behind the building a few minutes later. As she parked, she noticed Sarah had already parked and was getting a couple of bags out of the back of her SUV. Trish walked over to help her.

Sarah hugged Trish, pushing her long brown bangs out of her face. "I hardly slept last night. I was so excited about the Grand Opening, and in my mind, I kept mentally crossing items off the long list of 'Things-to-Do.' I guess we are finally ready for the opening."

When she arrived at the door, Sarah stepped back and looked at Trish, "I think you should have the honor of unlocking the door on this special morning."

Getting her key out of her pocket, Trish walked up to the back door, inserted it into the lock, turned it to the right, and started to push on the door. But she abruptly stopped and pulled the key out of the door.

Sarah was so close behind Trish she bumped into her. "What's wrong, Trish? Why did you stop?"

"Shh….be quiet. I thought I heard something, like a crunching sound and some movement inside. I'm not sure we should open the door," Trish said in barely a whisper.

Both women stood completely still for a moment but didn't hear anything.

"I think maybe my imagination is working overtime. I've been overly excited about the Grand Opening. I don't hear anything now." Trish inserted the key back into the door, turned it to the right, and pushed it, and it opened easily as it typically did.

Trish reached inside to turn the lights on before stepping across the threshold. Cautiously peering inside, she saw everything looked fine. The two women slowly continued inside the building and into the storage room, turning on more lights.

Suddenly, Trish released a breath she didn't know she'd been holding. "Phew…everything seems to be in order.

Let's put our bags in the storage room and get the coffee going. Then we can set up the refreshments you brought. The delicious aroma coming from these bakery bags from The Perk is making me hungry."

After leaving the bags in the storage room, the two women walked down the hall and entered the newly renovated and decorated retail space.

Sarah reached over and flipped up the series of light switches, which created a flood of light throughout the retail space.

But, instead of seeing the organized and tidy room they left last night, what they saw caused them both to gasp.

Trish was the first to recover enough to speak, "Oh No. This is awful. I can't imagine what happened in here."

The scene before them brought tears to Trish's eyes. Items were pulled off shelves, hangers were empty, and their former garments were lying on the floor. One display case was shattered, and glass splinters were scattered across the floor. The lamp that previously sat on top of the display case was now lying across it, probably the cause of the glass shattering.

Trish grabbed Sarah's arm. "We need to get out of here. Someone could still be inside."

The two women ran back down the hallway and out the back door, stopping a few feet from the bottom step, and stood silently for a few seconds, not wanting to admit they were scared. Finally, Trish took a few steps back toward the door and relocked it so no one could run outside where they were standing. Her hands trembled as she turned the key.

Pulling her phone out of her jacket pocket, Trish dialed 911. "This is Trish Cavanaugh, owner of Crystal Lake Gifts at 300 Main Street. Someone broke into our store overnight… yes, we relocked the back door. We're in the alley behind the store." Trish listened again to the 911 dispatcher. Trish disconnected the call and turned around to tell Sarah what the dispatcher had instructed them to do. "We're to go to the front of the store, where it's more visible, and wait for the police."

The two women hurried around the corner to the front of the store.

Several minutes later, two Lewisville Police Cars came speeding down the street with flashing lights and sirens blaring. One car pulled up to the front of the store, and one headed back to the alleyway which served Main and Pine Streets.

When the officer exited the police car, Trish was shocked to see Derrick Williams, her former high school crush, wearing the Chief of Police uniform. Obviously, Derrick was back in town. *He looks good in his dark blue uniform and Canadian Mounties-style hat.* Even though he was clean-shaven, his brown hair was a bit long at his neck, which made it curl up around the band on the hat. Somehow, Trish thought that looked sexy.

Trish realized she must be in shock. Her store had been robbed, and instead of worrying about what was stolen, she was daydreaming about the Chief of Police.

She quickly returned to reality when Chief Williams asked her for the front and back door keys. He told Trish and Sarah to move back behind his police car and stay put. With his gun drawn, Chief Williams unlocked the door and cautiously walked inside the store.

Through the window, Trish watched as he walked the entire length of the store, and then she saw the other officer, who had entered from the back, meet the Chief near the front checkout counter. She saw them put their service weapons away, and the Chief motioned for Trish and Sarah to join them inside.

"Luckily, whoever was here had already left, although it's odd neither the front nor the back door lock was damaged. Who has keys to the store beside the two of you?" Chief Williams asked.

Trish spoke up first. "No one. Once the renovations were completed, the local locksmith changed the locks and gave us new keys. I'm confused. Are you saying whoever entered the store didn't break in but must have had a key?"

Chief Williams looked around at the damage before responding, "The locks were not damaged or pried open, and no windows were broken, but there is damage inside the store. The forensics team is on its way. They will dust for fingerprints and try to decide what happened. I'll need a list of your employees and contractors, and we'll investigate, but the situation seems a bit odd."

"Can we go inside and start cleaning up the mess? Today is our Grand Opening." Trish looked at the Chief with hopeful eyes.

"Not until we complete our investigation. Why don't you two ladies go to The Perk? I'll come over and let you know when you can come inside. And Trish, I'm sorry this happened. I know how hard you've been working on getting the renovations completed. I've seen you here late at night as I did my patrol of Main Street."

Trish and Sarah looked dismally at each other and realized they had no choice. The Grand Opening would need to be delayed. Trish reached into her shoulder briefcase and pulled out a large post-it note and a black marker. She wrote a message to stick on the door that the grand opening would be delayed and to check the store's website for updates.

The two women walked across the street and into The Perk, but before they could even sit down, they realized the entire shop was buzzing about what had happened at the store. Several people stopped by to speak with them, and the barista brought over their regular orders, saying they were on the house.

Tears ran down Trish's face, and she felt herself shaking. She needed to pull herself together. She looked over at Sarah, who was staring at her.

"Are you okay?" Sarah asked. "I know it was scary, but we are fine, and the damage didn't look extensive. I didn't notice anything missing, but we'll need to look deeper into that when we're allowed back inside the store. It's good you didn't set up the register last night. We have a big mess to clean up and some glass to replace, but it will be okay. Let's drink our coffee and take a few minutes to calm down."

Sarah changed the subject, obviously trying to take Trish's mind off the situation. "By the way, I recall you and Chief Williams were an item in high school. Have you reconnected with him since he's been back in town?"

"No. I've seen Derrick around town, but we haven't spoken. I've avoided running into him a few times when I was getting coffee at The Perk. We did date in high school, but it didn't end well, and it was an embarrassing situation for us. I don't think either of us wants to relive those days."

"What happened in high school? Why would you avoid running into him?"

Trish was lost in thought for a minute before responding. "It was our senior year, and we'd been going steady for months. We were inseparable. Derrick was the football team's captain, a big thing in a small town like Lakeview. Our senior prom was coming up, and I assumed Derrick would ask me to go as his date. I told everyone I was going with the captain of the football team. I worked hard to save enough money to buy a gorgeous gown and matching shoes. But he never asked me. Finally, two weeks before the prom, one of the popular boys at school asked me to be his date, and I said yes."

There was a brief pause, and then Trish continued her story, "When Derrick heard I was going with someone else, he came to see me. He was so hurt. He asked why I dumped him. I told him I didn't, but I wanted to go to the prom—it was every girl's dream to attend her senior prom—and he hadn't invited me.

"With his head hanging down, he explained the situation and told me he had to wait to ask me because he didn't have the money for the tickets or the dinner. He was working overtime and trying to save enough money, but since it was only him and his mom, he also had to help out financially at home.

"He should have told me, but said he was embarrassed and didn't think I would understand. I was so mad he didn't think I would have understood. Had he thought so little of me? At that point, we got into a terrible argument and said things we didn't really mean. And then I made a bad judgment call and went to the prom with the other guy. It ended up being a terrible night, and I regretted my decision. My date was a total jerk, and he bragged to his friends that he stole me away from the captain of the football team. Finally, I couldn't take anymore and asked him to drive me home. He was not happy, and neither was I."

Trish paused, cleared her throat, and added, "Derrick and I never spoke again. A few months later, I heard he got an academic scholarship to the University of Maine and left town. I never saw him again until he moved back a few months ago. I'm not sure I can face him. Now do you understand why I've been avoiding him?"

"That was many years ago, and you were both teenagers. Don't you think Derrick has forgotten about the situation or at least gotten over it?" Sarah answered.

Before Trish could respond, she saw Cassidy and Amanda rushing into the coffee shop.

"Are you two all right?" Cassidy practically shouted. "We heard the news, and even though we heard you were okay, we had to see for ourselves. What happened?"

Trish looked at her two friends and tried to figure out how they had heard about the robbery so quickly, but it was a small town, and local news and gossip traveled faster than 5G wireless. "We're fine. Sit down, and we'll bring you up to speed on everything."

An hour later, Chief Williams called Trish on her cell phone and told her they were done with their initial probe but had no leads on what had happened. He informed her they could return to the shop and clean up the mess. He promised he would keep in touch as he continued his investigation.

Small-town residents were known for pulling together to help each other, and Lakeview was no different. With the help of dozens of friends, family, and other merchants on Main Street, the shop was cleaned up and repairs were made. Unfortunately, replacing the glass for the display case and adding a burglar alarm delayed the opening for an entire week.

CHAPTER SIX

The rescheduled Grand Opening was a bright and sunny day. The big front display windows allowed light to flood the store, and every surface gleamed. The shelves were neatly stocked, garments hung properly on the racks, and music quietly played from the hidden speakers.

Due to the break-in, the Grand Opening of Crystal Lake Gifts received a lot of additional interest and publicity, and Trish was prepared for heavy sales on Monday morning. In addition, Cassidy and Amanda took a day away from Crystal Lake Inn and arrived at the shop ready to support their best friend.

Trish gave Amanda, Cassidy, and Sarah outfits from her new clothing line as a thank-you gift. Each woman wore a different outfit, which had been hand-picked specifically for the wearer. It was a terrific way to show off the new line.

"You all look fabulous!" Trish called out to her friends. "This will be a wonderful start to our new endeavor, and not only are you helping the store run smoothly today, but you're also acting as models for the new clothing line. I'm so excited to launch Lakeview Designs. I hope you like the new name. I wanted to keep it simple and easy for people to remember. I was up late last night updating our website to include the new line. I can't wait to make my first sale. It will be interesting to see if it's online or in the shop. Fingers crossed, the line does well."

Looking at her watch, she continued, "We have about thirty minutes before we open the doors. Plenty of coffee and donuts are in the breakroom. Why don't you take a break before we open? Sarah and I need to prepare the registers and get the credit card machine started." And with those words, Trish motioned for Sarah to join her at the checkout counter.

As Trish got close to the counter, the lights flickered, and a second later, everything went dark. There were no lights, no music, nothing. The red glare from the emergency exit signs was the only light visible. Thankfully, the sun coming in through the front windows allowed the women to see what they were doing.

"What the heck happened now?" Trish yelled across the room and hurried to the back of the store where the electrical box was located. She opened the metal door and looked at the array of buttons. They all seemed to be where she thought they should be. She wiggled a few, but nothing happened. By now, they were down to twenty-five minutes until opening, and of course, they couldn't open without electricity. It could be dangerous in the darker corners, and they wouldn't have any way to ring up sales. *Why is this happening?* It seemed they were doomed.

The five women gathered around the electrical box like they could magically wish the electricity back on. Trish quickly walked to the front window to see if the electricity was off at other shops along Main Street, but she could see lights in several stores. In addition, The Perk had lights, and the stoplights were working.

Cassidy spoke up, "Trish, you need to call your electrician. Didn't you use the same person for your store renovations as I did for the renovations at the inn? I'm sure he'll come quickly under the circumstances."

"Just my luck. Mr. Powell sold his electrical business to a new guy, and as soon as my initial renovations were finished, he and his wife retired and moved to Florida to be closer to their grandkids." Trish placed her hands on her hips in frustration. "I haven't met the new owner, but Mr. Powell gave me his card."

Walking to the counter, Trish pulled a business card out of the drawer. "His name is Tom Spencer. I'll call him right now."

Trish pulled her phone out of her pocket and punched in the phone number listed on the business card, "Mr. Spencer, this is Trish Cavanaugh from Crystal Lake Gifts. Mr. Powell gave me your card and said you purchased his electrical business. Today is the Grand Opening of our shop on Main Street. We open in twenty minutes, and we don't have any electricity. Is there any way you could come here immediately? I've already had one delay to our opening, and I expect a large turnout today."

The look on Trish's face made it clear the call wasn't going as she had hoped. "I understand you have other work scheduled today, but this is an emergency. I would appreciate it if you could come now. I can't wait until tomorrow."

After a few moments of silence, Trish smiled, "Thank you so much, Mr. Spencer. It's Crystal Lake Gifts, located at 300 Main Street, across from The Perk. I'll be waiting at the front door for you."

Trish looked at the four women staring at her. How could this be happening? At least the electrician agreed to come right away. Maybe they could still salvage their Grand Opening.

Five minutes later, a white work van with Lakeview Electrical Service printed on the side pulled into a spot in front of the shop. After grabbing a toolbox, two men came to the door. Trish quickly introduced herself.

The taller man spoke up, "I'm Tom Spencer, the new owner of Lakeview Electrical Service, and this young man is an apprentice from the local technical school and is working with me part-time. Direct us to your electrical box." Tom motioned to the shorter man to follow him.

As Tom walked past Trish, she noticed the back of his tee shirt. She had to hide a giggle rising from her chest. It read, Lakeview Electrical Services…We Light You Up. She also noticed Tom had a muscular build and wondered if he worked out at the local gym. Standing over six feet tall with big brown eyes and big pecs, he was a handsome man.

She returned her attention to the conversation when she realized Tom was speaking to her. "What seems to be the problem?" When Trish didn't respond, he looked over at the other woman standing next to Trish.

Sarah let out a slow breath before eventually speaking, "Since we are standing in the dark, I think the problem should be clear. Our electricity is out. We looked at the 'thingies' in the gray box, but they are all in the right position. We should be opening in fifteen minutes, but can't open without electricity. Can you do something to get the electricity back on?"

"Mr. Spencer, let me introduce you to Sarah Cavanaugh." Trish jumped into the conversation to make introductions and smooth over the unexpectedly harsh tone from Sarah. "She heads up the local artisans' community and is now selling a variety of handmade goods in the shop. Today's opening is as important to her group as it is to me."

Tom Spencer glanced at Sarah with a look of amusement, but instead of responding, he opened his toolbox, pulled out a few tools, including a flashlight, and opened the metal electrical box. After clicking several switches back and forth a few times, he dug around for a few more tools and removed the cover and the front frame from the electrical box.

When he pulled the outer cover away from the box, a pile of acorns poured out of the wall. "What the heck?" Tom gasped. "It looks like these acorns got behind some of the circuit breakers. I think I can repair this in a few minutes. If you ladies would give us room to work on the…umm… 'thingies'," he briefly hesitated, "that would be helpful." He grinned and winked at Sarah.

Trish and Sarah walked back to the front of the shop and told the others what they saw. Fortunately, with only five minutes to spare, the electricity was restored.

Tom came over to where Sarah was standing. "It looks like there was a small opening in the wall behind the electrical box, and some type of small animal used it to store its acorns. Eventually, the sharp edges of the broken acorns started to cut into one of the wires. Fortunately, I was able to fix it. I looked around, but I didn't see any nests. So, those shells could have been in the wall for years. I put some insulation behind the box, which should stop any interference for now, but I think you should consider replacing the entire unit. It's outdated, and this could keep happening."

Trish and Sarah exchanged worried looks, but neither immediately spoke up.

Tom continued. "I read the note that your former electrician left me regarding future service needed on this facility. He recommended that you upgrade the entire electrical system soon. Also, when you added the new alarm system, you used the last available circuit, so you will be limited in adding more electrical appliances. I can estimate the job later, but you should be fine with opening the shop for now. I'll send you the bill."

And with that, Tom turned around, nodded to all of the women, took one last smug look at Sarah, and quickly left the shop. But Trish noticed electricity in the air between Tom and Sarah, and the sparks were not from the electrical box.

Once Tom stowed his tools in the truck and sent his helper to The Perk to grab two cups of coffee for the road, he had time to replay the scene in the shop. He quickly realized that Sarah was the same woman he'd seen at the Lakeview Farmers Market a few weeks earlier. He remembered being mesmerized by her emerald-green eyes—he didn't recall ever seeing eyes that exact same color. She was a natural beauty who didn't wear makeup and still looked gorgeous.

He chuckled when he thought about how she explained the circuits as 'thingies.' That was a first for him and reminded him there seemed to be some type of current between them. Just like when he was working with live wires, he needed to remind himself he could get burned getting into a relationship with someone who seemed to reach a boiling point so quickly.

His helper returned and put a stop to his daydreaming for now, but he was sure more thoughts of Sarah and those darn emerald-green eyes would be back to visit him.

CHAPTER SEVEN

It only took a few minutes to finalize everything, and at ten o'clock sharp, Trish unlocked the front door and turned the beautiful, hand-painted sign, dangling on a bright white silk ribbon, from CLOSED to OPEN.

Sales were brisk, and there was significant interest in the homemade items from LACE and the new Lakeview Designs clothing line. All four women stayed busy assisting customers and stocking shelves. The morning flew by quickly.

Trish had lunch delivered for the team, and they took turns taking breaks to be sure no customers were left waiting. Around two o'clock, Trish looked up to see an elderly couple looking at the small selection of baby clothes, so she walked over to see if she could help them.

"Hi, I'm Trish. I noticed you were looking at those adorable sundresses. Can I help you with anything?"

"Thank you for coming over to help us. Our daughter-in-law is expecting our second grandchild this summer, and I think this little pink dress is adorable. It would be perfect as a gift for the upcoming baby shower. We are the Connellys. We're guests at Crystal Lake Inn, where we stay every year for a family vacation. Cassidy recommended we stop by your shop. It's absolutely lovely, exactly like she said."

Hearing her name mentioned, Cassidy walked over to Mr. and Mrs. Connelly, "It's so nice to see you. I'm glad you decided to stop by the shop today. I see you found that adorable sundress I mentioned we were stocking on the shelves. There's also a little pair of pink socks with white ruffles and a beautiful white sweater on the next rack," Cassidy said as she guided the couple to the following table.

Cassidy rang up the sales, wrapped the gift, and walked Mr. and Mrs. Connelly to the door, thanking them again for stopping by.

"Cassidy, thank you for sending your guests from the inn to the shop. I love free advertising." Trish returned to the checkout counter with Cassidy.

Trish lowered her voice, "Maybe it's me, but did you feel the sparks between Tom and Sarah this morning? It's been a long time since I've seen Sarah react like that toward a man. Tom is new in town. Do you know anything about him?"

Cassidy kept her voice low. "I saw Tom at the last Lakeview Merchants Association meeting. He introduced himself and said he bought the business from Mr. Powell. He also mentioned he has some relatives nearby but didn't mention their names. I'll keep my ears open and let you know if I hear anything else."

The remainder of the day went smoothly, but everyone breathed a sigh of relief when Trish twisted the sign on the front door to CLOSED.

Trish turned to the group. "I can't thank you enough. Today wouldn't have been possible without your help. We exceeded our sales expectations. Cassidy and Amanda, I know you need to return to the inn. It's fine to finish what you're doing and leave for the day. Sarah and I can do a bit of restocking, and I'll head back to the inn once we lock up."

I'm confident Sarah and I can handle the shop for the remainder of the week. On Saturday, two girls from the local high school are coming in to help us." Trish sighed and then smiled. "Thanks for making our dreams become a reality." She gave each of her friends a big hug.

An hour later, everyone had left the shop except Trish, who had stayed behind. She walked around the shop, straightened a few items, and looked out the big front windows. She could see people hurrying down the street while a few couples slowly strolled along the sidewalk, probably heading to dinner at one of the Main Street restaurants.

Seeing the couples holding hands or quietly talking while waiting outside for their reservations reminded Trish how long it had been since she'd had a special man in her life. Thinking about relationships pushed her thoughts to Derrick. She wondered if he was still single. Was he seeing someone these days? *He sure looked good in his uniform.*

As if thinking about him magically made him appear, she noticed his patrol car heading toward her shop. She realized she was excited to see Chief Williams again, only to watch him drive past her shop and continue down Main Street. She saw his taillights disappear around the corner.

Looking back over her shoulder at the beautiful shop, she smiled. She was so fortunate to have her dreams come true. So why look for trouble or disappointment? She had enough on her plate.

Trish walked over to the check-out counter, reached down to the storage area, grabbed her purse, and turned off the lights as she walked to the back door.

Before stepping outside, she looked at the gray electrical box. The entire acorn thing was a mystery, but one that would have to wait for another day. Trish was tired, her feet hurt, and she was dying to return to the inn and join the gang for the nightly Sit-n-Sip on the front porch.

The nightly gathering on the inn's front porch was a relaxing way to shift gears from a busy day and enjoy the beautiful surroundings. The large porch wrapped around three sides of the inn and provided ample places for guests to sit, talk, and watch the sun move lower over the lake, creating bursts of color.

The nightly Sit-n-Sip was also the best place to catch up with her friends, find out the local gossip, and maybe…just maybe…see if anyone had anything to say about a certain local police chief.

CHAPTER EIGHT

"Can I speak to Chief Williams, please? This is Trish Cavanaugh." The hold music was pleasant, but Trish wasn't willing to listen to it for long. She was frustrated, which, in turn, was making her irritable.

"I'm sorry, but Chief Williams is not available right now. He's on a conference call for another hour. He said he would call you in the morning since it's so late in the day." The person who answered the phone never bothered to identify who she was.

"Okay. Please tell Chief Williams it's important I speak to him as soon as possible." Trish hung up the phone, even more frustrated than before she had made the call.

Yesterday, Trish received a letter from the insurance company. It said they wouldn't make payments until they got the final police report that provided the official conclusion.

Trish had been using the same insurance company for the six years she'd been in business and had only made one minor claim in all that time. But now, when she needed them to reimburse her for the recent damage to her store, it was one delay after another. It had been several weeks since the incident, and her agent seemed to be dragging his feet.

Chief Williams said the report was filed with the insurance company the previous week. Still, when Trish got her copy in the mail earlier today, she realized the section where the official conclusion should be listed only stated the investigation was inconclusive. That was not helpful at all.

Leaving the letter on the counter, Trish walked into the breakroom to fix a cup of chamomile tea to help calm her nerves. As she waited for the water to heat, she noticed several cookie crumbs on the counter which she wiped off with a paper towel. She saw two empty cookie wrappers on the floor, picked them up, and threw them into the trashcan. It wasn't like her staff to be so messy. She needed to address this with the team.

Since it was after hours, Trish finished her tea at the checkout counter. She wanted to walk around the store again before leaving for the night. Trish stopped to straighten a few items, refolded the baby tee shirts to make a cuter display, and refilled a couple of empty spots on the new Lakeview tee shirts rack. Once everything looked tidy, she turned off the lights and headed down the hallway to grab her purse.

Before getting to the back door, she was thrust into darkness and the ear-splitting sound of the burglar alarm going off. Feeling her way along the hallway wall, Trish found the entrance into the breakroom, opened a drawer, and grabbed one of the flashlights kept in case of an emergency.

Trish was reasonably sure no one was in the store except for her, but her heart was pounding. She walked back into the main showroom, which was empty. She wandered through the entire shop and checked that all the doors were locked. She finally realized it must be a false alarm caused by another fault in the electrical system. She took her phone from the pocket of her slacks and quickly called the alarm company so they would not call the local police department. She didn't need another lecture from Chief Williams. She was tired and needed to get to the inn to eat dinner, take a long bath, and get a good night's sleep. *I can't believe how tired I am.*

A few days later, another strange alarm-related scene occurred. Trish had been at the checkout counter, getting ready to open the shop for the day. The overhead lights flashed a few times, and the cash register's digital display flashed wildly. But it all only lasted a few seconds before returning to normal. Trish completed her morning routine and started across the room to unlock the front door when she saw a police car speeding down Main Street. Of course, she was curious about where it was headed, only to see the patrol vehicle stop right in front of her store. She was even more shocked to see Chief Williams get out of the car, run to her door, and gesture for her to open the shop door quickly.

"Derrick, what in the world are you doing? You scared me half to death." Trish was out of breath due to her nerves, which came close to making her hyperventilate.

"Are you okay? Is everything all right? Is anyone else in the store?" Derrick questioned.

"Of course, I'm all right. What is going on, and why are you here?"

"Your silent alarm went off, and I happened to be headed down Main Street when the call came in, so I decided to respond. Are you sure you're not in any danger?"

Trish cocked her head to one side and, without realizing it, put her hands on her hips. "Of course I'm okay. I'm the only one here. I didn't push the panic alarm. Sarah doesn't arrive for another hour. We only have one panic alarm, and it's under the checkout counter. I didn't touch anything. I think there's some issue with the system."

Trish was interrupted from making further comments as her cell phone started to ring. The alarm company called to inform her the panic alarm went off due to an electrical malfunction. No one pushed the button. It was a precaution built into the system so that anyone cutting the electric flow to the security system would automatically trigger an alert to the police. In this case, a short in the electrical system triggered the panic alarm.

Yet again, Trish was embarrassed in front of Derrick when she relayed the information.

Derrick smiled at Trish. "It's okay, and I'm glad you aren't in any danger. The problem is your new security system has already experienced two false alarms. The city ordinance calls for merchants to be fined after three accidental alarms. It takes our meager resources away from keeping our citizens safe. I want to be here if you need me, but if it's another false alarm, you're taking me away from others who need my assistance."

Trish quietly responded, "I'm so sorry, Derrick. I'm trying to get the electrical issues resolved. Let's hope this is the last false alarm."

Neither spoke for a minute, but Trish could feel a spark of attraction between them. She wasn't sure if the 'electricity' had come from her or Derrick or both of them, but when he started to take a step closer to her, his police radio went off, and he had another emergency to get to.

After Derrick was gone, she suddenly felt alone. She started to think about her high school years and what might have been if the situation had been different. *But wishful thinking doesn't change the past.*

It was starting to feel like Groundhog Day. A few weeks later, Trish was once again jolted by the wail of police sirens and flashing red lights. Looking up through the store's front window, she sucked in a deep breath. Staring at her through the front window was Chief Williams. She yelled through the window that another momentary electrical outage must have caused a false alarm.

She saw Derrick walk back to his police car and back, then unfold a piece of paper, taping it on the window with the writing side tightly pressed against the pane.

Moving closer to the window so Trish could read the writing, she realized it was a citation for having her third false alarm and calling out the Lakeview Police Department, thus potentially putting other residents at risk. The fine was two-hundred-and-fifty dollars.

Trish unlocked the front door to let Derrick inside.

"Derrick, I'm so sorry about the false alarm. It's the same electrical issue we've been experiencing. I'm sure you can understand and not give me a fine this time. It has been a nightmare for both of us."

She cleared her throat. "And I've been trying to get in touch with you, so now that you're here, can we talk about the lack of determination by the police department regarding how the vandalism in my store on the first day occurred?"

Trish hoped to change the subject and get Derrick to overlook the third false alarm. She walked over to the checkout counter, retrieved the latest letter from the insurance company, and handed it to Derrick.

"Trish, I can't overlook the citation. The court clerk generated the violation citation and had it on file. You'll have to take that up at the Courthouse in the morning. Regarding the first incident, since nothing was missing and none of the doors or windows were broken, the only conclusion is that the mess inside was caused by someone with a key. I think it's best to leave it at that and deal with the insurance company as best you can." He shifted uncomfortably. "I'm sorry Trish, but I can't offer any other solutions," Derrick said, then walked out the door, got into his squad car, and left.

Trish was furious but realized Derrick was right. She knew what she had to do. First thing in the morning, she'd get Tom Spencer on the phone and push for the upgraded electrical system to be installed as soon as possible. Next, she'd call the insurance company and start the process of disputing their decision not to reimburse her for the damage.

Finally, she'd forget Derrick Williams ever existed. He had broken her heart once before. She was a smart and savvy businesswoman and typically made sound judgment calls. She needed to consider her past with Derrick and stay clear of future heartbreak. On the other hand, he looked so sexy in his police uniform. Maybe her hormones were clouding her judgment when it came to Chief Williams. She needed to get some fresh air and clear her head.

She grabbed her purse and keys and walked out the back door. Taking a deep breath, she started her car and drove back to the inn.

Trish parked in her usual spot behind the inn and exited her car, intending to head inside. But the glistening of the setting sun over the lake drew her attention, and she walked down to the water's edge. It was a view she couldn't imagine ever getting tired of seeing. This time of day was gorgeous, with light orange, purple, and blue tints slightly rippling across the water.

She was alone. Everyone had gone back to their homes or out to dinner. The sounds of nature were all around her, and Trish could smell a hint of something delicious coming from the inn. She wondered what Peter had prepared for dinner. Although she was hungry, she decided to take a quick walk along the lake's edge to take in the beautiful scenery.

Sitting on one of the benches by the lake, Trish realized her entire body was still tense from the earlier scene with Derrick. She needed to calm down and let her body and mind relax. She took several deep breaths using deep breathing exercises she learned in a yoga class years ago. Breathe in and hold it for four seconds. Exhale and count to four. Inhale and hold it for four seconds. Exhale and count to four. By the end of the fourth exhale, she was already feeling more peaceful.

Trish watched the sun lower itself until it finally hid behind the horizon. There would be time in the morning to stew over the dreadful situation of the past few hours. Tonight, she'd sit serenely and watch the scene that nature played each night as the final rays of sunlight danced across the lake.

CHAPTER NINE

"I've checked my schedule, and if I move a few jobs around, I can start your work on Sunday," Tom Spencer told Trish. "Since you're only open a few hours on Sunday afternoons, we can work more efficiently than maneuvering around customers all day. We'll also work nights right after you close. We'll finish the rewiring in two weeks if the work goes well. Is that okay with you?"

Trish breathed a sigh of relief, "Yes, that would be wonderful. I was worried it would take longer and also disrupt our business. Sarah and I talked about it, and she offered to be here so she can cover the merchandise in the areas where you and your team are working each night and uncover them again when you leave. This will allow us to keep the store open and make all merchandise available to our customers."

"Sounds good. I've hired two additional electricians for this job. We'll see Sarah on Sunday morning at seven a.m. sharp," Tom added.

Before Trish could say goodbye, Tom hung up the phone. She was starting to think the entire town needed a lesson in phone etiquette. When did people get so rude?

Trish walked to the front sales floor to find Sarah and give her an update. The two had already discussed the situation, and Sarah offered to work the odd hours when the workers were there. This would allow her to catch up on replenishing some of her stock. The merchandise was selling better than they expected, and while this was a good problem, it still added to the stress of the other issues the shop was experiencing.

Sarah seemed hesitant about the potential of spending so much time with Tom Spencer, although when Trish asked her about it, she said she was okay with the arrangement.

Trish wondered if something was brewing between Tom and Sarah, good or bad. Either way, Trish was going to keep an eye on the situation. Something was bothering Sarah, or at least that was the feeling Trish got every time she brought up Tom Spencer's name.

Sunday morning arrived, and so did a bright blue sky. It would be a beautiful day, and Sarah was trying not to feel sorry for herself for having to work inside on her day off.

The town was quiet on Sunday mornings at six-forty-five, but you could bet at least a few customers would already be at The Perk. As Sarah entered the shop, the aroma of strong coffee and fresh-baked blueberry muffins beckoned her to the counter. She thought it would be an excellent way to get the rewiring job off to a good start if she treated the workers to freshly baked muffins and an assortment of donuts. Then, she'd make coffee for them in their breakroom.

"Hello, Sarah. I'm surprised to see you here on a Sunday morning. What's up?" Amy Holden owned The Perk, and she typically took the Sunday early morning shift to give her regular staff time off to attend church with their families.

"The rewiring job starts today. We've hired Lakeview Electrical. Tom Spencer took over the company when the former owner retired and moved to Florida to be closer to his grandchildren. The team plans to work evenings and the next two Sundays, so don't be surprised if you see lights on at Crystal Lake Gifts after our regular hours," Sarah responded.

"I'm so happy you could get the job moved up. Whenever the alarm goes off at your shop, my customers run outside to see what's happening. If it keeps up, I may have to charge you and Trish a service fee," Amy laughed. "These old buildings are costly to keep up, but once you get all the major stuff done, they're wonderful, and it's great to see the expansion of Trish's shop. It helps all the merchants on Main Street because of the extra foot traffic."

Amy walked over to grab her order pad. "What can I get you today? I have fresh blueberry muffins and apple fritters if you're interested?"

"You read my mind. I'll take six of each. I need to keep the guys fed so they keep working."

Amy placed all the items in a large shopping bag and handed it to Sarah. "Let me know if you need anything else. We close at three o'clock today, but if you want to order any takeout, be sure to call me by two o'clock and I'll have one of the staff bring it over to you before we close."

"You're so thoughtful. I appreciate the offer and will check with the guys and let you know. But I've got to hurry and unlock the doors before they beat them down. Thanks again." Sarah hurried across the street.

She unlocked the front door to the shop, but before she stepped inside, Sarah stopped and noticed how beautiful the hanging baskets looked and how the rainbow of colors added to the ambiance of Main Street. Once inside, she turned to relock the door and headed to the breakroom. Putting down the bag, she went to the back door and unlocked it. She opened it slightly to see if any workers were waiting for her, but the alley was empty.

Sarah went to the breakroom and started the coffee. Next, she put a fresh tablecloth on the breakroom table, placed some muffins and fritters on a large platter, and added napkins and a few hand-painted dessert plates.

Before leaving for work, Sarah had picked some lovely geraniums growing in her garden. She wrapped them in damp paper towels, grabbed a simple vase, and put everything in a reusable bag. She had planned to put them on the checkout counter at the shop. But wanting the table to look festive, she grabbed the vase, placed the flowers in it, and sat it on the table. She surprised herself and suddenly realized she wanted to make a good impression on Tom.

Standing back to see how the display looked, she nodded her approval and went to finish the coffee set-up.

Sarah finished filling up a coffee carafe to start another pot, assuming the workers would need several cups to get them going when she heard a noise behind her. Startled, she quickly turned around, swinging the full carafe like a weapon at whatever moved behind her.

Thankfully, she had a lousy aim and narrowly missed hitting Tom Spencer in the head.

"TOM! You scared the living daylights out of me. I didn't hear you come in."

"I'm so sorry, Sarah. I assumed you heard me and the guys come in when we dropped our toolboxes in the backroom. The crew went back outside to carry in a load of supplies, and I smelled the coffee. I thought I'd grab a few cups for the guys."

Suddenly, Sarah realized Tom had stepped forward and was intently staring at her. He froze but quickly started speaking to cover up the uncomfortable moment. "I'm sorry I scared you. And the table looks beautiful, but you realize these workers will be lugging miles of electrical wire through this room. I'm worried they will break those delicate little plates. Do you have any paper plates?"

Sarah's heart started wildly beating in her chest. *Why is Tom staring at me so intently?* Her body involuntarily leaned forward to reduce the space between them. It took her a minute to register what Tom had said. Finally, the fog cleared and Sarah straightened up and said, "Pardon me, did you insult my lovely table? After nearly scaring me to death, you could at least appreciate my effort for you and your team. I don't understand men." She was joking, of course, but somehow, it didn't land humorously. She watched his face turn red, and she wanted to take it back.

Pulling paper plates from the cabinet, Sarah handed them to Tom. "Please tell the guys they can help themselves to the food and coffee. There are more muffins in the box on the counter. If you need me, I'll be in my workroom on the other side of this wall."

Sarah marched out of the room in a huff, partially from embarrassment and partly to hide her reaction to Tom.

Once she got to her crafting room, she closed the door and leaned against it. Sarah wasn't sure why she had reacted so strongly to Tom's comment. But, in thinking it through, he was right. As much as Tom said the team would try to avoid large-scale messes, drilling through walls with hundred-year-old plaster would be dusty, and the guys didn't have time to be careful with delicate china.

What was I thinking? Duh, I guess I wasn't thinking clearly. There's something about being around Tom that makes me lose my perspective. I've got to get my act together. I've embarrassed myself, yet again, in front of him. This is the last time it's going to happen.

She shook her head to clear it and sat at the table to finish some delicate stitching on the binding of a Double Wedding Ring quilt. It was a special order, and she had promised to deliver it later this week. She still had about ten hours of work to do on it.

As Sarah unfolded the quilt, she was reminded of the complexity of this specific pattern, a traditional quilt for newlyweds because of the interlocking circles, which represented a life-long unity. It took thousands of tiny pieces of fabric sewn into interlocking rings across the entire quilt. In the center of each circle, stitching was used to form the shape of a heart, only visible when you looked closely. Overall, the quilt's beauty and the tender-loving care put into it by the original quilter shined through. The person who ordered it was giving it to their youngest daughter for her wedding shower. It would make a wonderful gift and turn into a family keepsake.

Sarah reached into her treasured antique sewing basket, pulled out the appropriate thread color, a needle, and a thimble to protect her finger, and got to work.

Several hours went by, and the crew was making good progress. Since the older store had been a large showroom with a small storage area, it was perfect for the artisans to use as their crafting room. The limited number of walls and exposed ceiling also made running the new electrical wires easier than expected.

Tom decided to grab lunch for the crew, walked across the street to The Perk, and asked to speak to the manager. He wanted to tell her he had a large job across the street and would buy his crew lunch and snacks. In addition, he wanted to check on the hours of operations and was hoping to open an account so any of his crew could come over and pick up their orders.

"Hi, I'm Amy. I own the coffee shop. How can I help you?"

"Hi, I'm doing a job across the street." Before he could continue, Amy interrupted him.

"Ahh, Mr. Spencer, welcome to The Perk."

Tom stopped speaking and was surprised this stranger knew his name.

Seeing his look of surprise, she said, "First, you must be new in town. I don't think I've seen you in my shop before. Second, Lakeview is a small town, and news travels fast. Third, Sarah was in here early this morning to buy treats for your crew, and told me about the project and that I might see lights on in the evening and on Sundays." Amy handed him a brochure. "Welcome to Lakeview, Mr. Spencer. I'll be happy to open an account for you."

"Call me Tom, please. I appreciate your help."

Amy was always curious about new merchants in Lakeview. "Do you have any relatives in Lakeview? What made you choose our wonderful little town?"

"Yes, my sister and her family live here, and when I saw an ad for someone to take over Lakeview Electrical, it seemed like the perfect opportunity."

Looking at the menu, Tom picked several sandwiches and snacks and told Amy he'd return in fifteen minutes to pick up his order.

At noon, the crew sat in the breakroom to enjoy lunch and take a break. After thanking Tom for the sandwiches, the guys talked about what they planned to accomplish before quitting around four o'clock. Once they agreed on the work plan, they cleaned up the mess in the breakroom and returned to work.

Tom had his head buried in paperwork and decided to stay in the breakroom. He realized he hadn't seen Sarah all morning. He hadn't meant to offend her earlier in the day. It had been thoughtful of her to set up the breakfast for the crew, but in all his years in the business, he never recalled a client using real china for a bunch of electricians. Oh, he could dress up in a tux for special events, and he knew the correct piece of silverware to use at a fancy table, but on the actual job, he'd never seen linen used before.

As if thinking about Sarah made her materialize, he saw her standing in front of the coffee pot. She looked nervous. He wasn't sure what, if anything, he should say. He walked over to the coffee pot to refill his mug. "Sarah. I want to apologize again for my comments this morning. You were so thoughtful, and the crew wanted me to thank you for the treats. It was a great way to start the job. It got the men going, and we are slightly ahead of schedule, so thanks again." Tom didn't know what else to say, so he looked back at his paperwork.

"I'm not sure why I overreacted," Sarah said softly. "I guess I was overthinking the situation. I'm typically a practical person. I'm glad the crew enjoyed the treats. I noticed that you got them lunch from The Perk. I hope they enjoyed it. I had planned to do that originally, but after the china incident, I thought it was better to leave it to you. I'm sure that Amy will appreciate the extra business."

"I met Amy. Thank you for letting her know about the project. She agreed to let me set up a tab so the crew wouldn't starve. And yes, the guys enjoyed their lunch. The sandwiches from The Perk are much better than the PB&J they typically bring from home."

As Tom turned back toward the table, he accidentally brushed Sarah's arm, and was surprised to feel a slight tingle. He saw the look on her face and realized Sarah also felt something between them. Maybe it was another power surge in the building…or perhaps, it was something else.

"I need to go check on the crew. Thanks for the fresh coffee." Tom couldn't get out of the room fast enough.

What was going on? He was a contented bachelor and intended to stay that way for a long time.

Yet, there was something special about Sarah. Even before he knew her name or who she was, those dark emerald eyes and long braided hair drew him in. And the way she stood up to him the first time they officially met. He recalled how she put her hands on her hips and tilted her head. *Was she the type of woman who could get under my skin?* His armor was cracking a little bit. He wasn't sure he was ready for it.

CHAPTER TEN

Typically, Trish loved Monday mornings. They brought the promise of a new week and the opportunity for new adventures. On this particular Monday morning though, the weather wasn't cooperating. Thunder and lightning storms had passed through the area around five o'clock that morning. The storms had moved out, but heavy rain continued to pelt down on Lakeview.

As Trish arrived at the store, she struggled to hold her umbrella against the rain while unlocking the back door. Luckily, they had installed a large canopy over the back door, which provided some protection from the weather.

Once inside, Trish went about her morning routine to open the store. With the most significant part of the rewiring job completed, she no longer crossed her fingers, hoping the alarm didn't go off. It had been a few weeks since she received and paid the fine for excessive false alarms. Thinking about it made her frown.

Rain continued to fall, and so did the sales at the shop. Rainy days were slower, so Trish kept busy rearranging displays. She had finished when a customer came into the shop. After picking out a few items, the customer came to the counter to check out. While Trish was wrapping the purchases for the birthday of the customer's grandchild, the woman mentioned when she was shopping on Main Street the prior week, she got a parking ticket from one of those fancy new parking meters. She swore she paid for an hour and was only parked for thirty minutes. She grumbled that getting the ticket made her rethink shopping on Main Street versus going to the mall a few miles away, where parking was free.

This wasn't the first time Trish heard a customer complain about getting a parking ticket, which they said was unjustified. "Time-expired" seemed to be the new term everyone used around town. The Lakeview Town Council had recently upgraded the old meters to all digital. The accuracy of the meters had been tested and approved by the Parking Enforcement Division of the Maine State Police.

When Trish had seen Derrick at The Perk a few days ago, she'd told him about the repeated customer complaints, but he had said his hands were tied. The Parking Enforcement Officers on his team had pictures of the expired time on the meters.

Later that same afternoon, once the rain stopped, Crystal Lake Gifts saw an increase in customers, so Trish forgot about the ticket problem until Cassidy stopped by the shop on her way to the Town Council meeting. Cassidy mentioned one of the topics on the agenda for the meeting was the new parking meters. She suggested Trish attend the meeting to see what other merchants had to say on the topic.

Leaving Sarah to close the shop, Trish headed to the Town Council meeting that evening.

The meeting was held in the Town Hall, which was in a restored two-story clapboard building. On either side of the steps leading to the front door were white columns and a porch large enough to hold several rocking chairs. Trish thought the best feature of the historical building was the attached clock tower, which still chimed every hour, thanks to the total refurbishment it received a few years ago.

Walking into the room, she saw twice as many Main Street merchants in attendance as usual. The long wooden pews were already packed, but fortunately, Cassidy had saved her a seat near the front of the room.

The Mayor banged an old wooden gavel on the podium and the room became quiet. He turned the meeting over to the Chairwoman of the Council, who got the meeting started.

When the Council had completed its standard agenda items, the issue of parking meters came up. A couple of merchants approached the podium and gave accounts of customers who complained about getting 'time-expired' tickets on the new parking meters. While they had a couple of specific examples, they failed to have any hard proof the meters were malfunctioning.

In frustration, Trish stood up to support the merchants who brought up the topic. She went up to the microphone and explained to the Council she also had a couple of customers complain. The Council reminded people the meters had been certified by the State Police and without proof they didn't have a case.

As a long-time member of the Town Council and the Merchants Association, Cassidy also spoke up about the issue. "We've worked so hard to drive traffic back to Main Street. Letting these ticket issues drive traffic away from Main Street would be a shame. Isn't there something we can do to validate the accuracy of the meters? Due to the negative impact already seen by some merchants, maybe we should consider removing them."

Before Cassidy finished speaking, the town busybody, Mrs. Lester, stood up and loudly protested the innkeeper's recommendation. The elderly woman, who always had her hair pulled back in a tight bun and perpetually wore a sweater, said the cost to have the meters validated again or removed would be too high for the town's taxpayers. The town had spent a fortune on the new automated meters.

"I'm pretty sure Mrs. Lester isn't even aware of the cost of the meters or how little the town is making from them," Trish whispered to Cassidy, who was seated next to her. Trish knew the contrary town gossip was known for speaking out at Council meetings about various topics, often without actual knowledge of the subject being discussed.

"I recently heard her complaining about hiring from outside of Lakeview for the Chief of Police role, even when Derrick was the most qualified candidate," Cassidy said.

Trish smiled to herself until she heard her name. "Ms. Cavanaugh, if you don't want your customers to pay for parking in front of your store, maybe you should consider reimbursing them," Mrs. Lester said snidely. "People have to pay for the privilege of parking right in front of the shops."

Several people nodded and grumbled, agreeing with Mrs. Lester, and the Chairwoman of the Council banged her gavel to regain control of the meeting.

The decision was made to keep the meters. However, the Council Chairwoman told the merchants the item would be added to the agenda for the next meeting if they wanted to bring back proof the meters were not working accurately. The meeting quickly adjourned. Several merchants gathered to discuss the situation. It was obvious they were unhappy. Cassidy suggested they should each try to get proof of the inaccurate meter readings and be prepared to share the evidence at the next Town Council Meeting.

Trish rose Sunday morning to a ray of sunshine sneaking through the crack in the drapes that covered the windows in her room at the inn. She got up and walked over to the window, pushing the drapes back to see the lake. It never failed to lift her spirits. The sun was barely up, but it was already glistening off the beautiful blue water.

Like most of the stores on Main Street, Crystal Lake Gifts didn't open until noon on Sunday, but with the rewiring job still underway, Sarah would be opening the store, leaving Trish to catch up on her laundry, sort through some paperwork, and grab a quick ride on her pretty red Triumph.

A short ride on her sweet little motorcycle was exactly what she needed after the hectic past few weeks. She quickly dressed in jeans and donned her leather jacket. Grabbing her helmet and gloves, Trish walked down the back stairs to the underground garage where her bike was stored. Opening the door, she was thrilled to see the gleaming motorcycle. She pushed her pink helmet onto her head, straddled the bike, hit the electronic starter, released the kickstand, and resisted the urge to gun the engine. Most guests would still be asleep at the inn, so she quietly rolled the bike out of the garage and down the back driveway.

CHAPTER ELEVEN

Trish took it slowly until she got away from the inn and town, then picked up speed as she hit US Route One. The coast roads were primarily empty this early on a Sunday morning, so she enjoyed the views of lakes, farms, and fields. After feeling the wind on her face for an hour, she stopped at a small coffee shop and grabbed a hot cup of java to warm her hands.

Looking at her watch, she realized she needed to head back to the inn if she wanted to help with the Sunday Brunch.

Trish jumped back on her bike and headed home, but not before a quick stop at one of the nearby state parks for a look at the historic Curtis Island Lighthouse. It was two-hundred years old and stood proudly on the coast, its light still working, although it no longer protected vessels from the storm.

The ride always settled her nerves and brought calm to her soul. She wondered why more people didn't ride motorcycles. You could leave your troubles behind you with each mile you traveled. Today's trip significantly reduced her anxiety level.

She was now ready to join her friends and help with the famous Crystal Lake Inn Sunday Brunch.

The brunch was extremely popular with guests at the inn and the town's residents. Peter never failed to create the most delectable menu possible.

Trish, Cassidy, and Amanda often used Sundays to catch up with each other, and the easiest way to do that was for Trish to help with the brunch. Cassidy and Amanda tried to get Trish to relax and enjoy the meal. But she loved working alongside her best friends, who now also included Cassidy's husband, Jack.

After quickly changing her clothes, Trish walked to the lobby, where she immediately smelled delicious aromas coming from the kitchen. Stopping to look at the large board that displayed the menu for today's brunch, she saw Peter's famous seafood quiche was the main attraction, along with crepes, several egg dishes, breakfast meats, and a waffle bar with every topping you could imagine. And, of course, mimosas were available to get your day off to a festive start.

Trish walked into the kitchen and saw Peter with a spatula in one hand and the other around Amanda's waist. Their lips were firmly locked together. She cleared her throat loudly to let the two know she was in the room, wondering if there would be wedding bells shortly.

"Hey, you two, break it up. Glancing at the reservation list on my way in here, it looks like we have a full house, and looking at the clock, we only have an hour to finish getting everything ready. I'll start getting the serving line set up. Can I trust the two of you to behave yourselves and get the cooking done?"

With a deep blush cascading down her neck, Amanda backed away from Peter. As she turned to walk away, Peter twisted the kitchen towel he quickly picked up from the counter and smacked Amanda on the butt.

"Ouch," Amanda yelled, but you could see the smile on her face. It was also easy to see she liked every minute of it.

"Okay, I'll get the fresh fruits and beverages out of the walk-in refrigerator and head into the dining room." Amanda quickly turned back toward Peter and added, "I'll deal with you later."

"I hope that's a promise," Peter replied as Amanda walked away.

Reaching the dining room, Trish looked around and smiled. She loved the way the inn was decorated. Cassidy had meticulously remodeled the inn, and each room was perfect. There was an excellent mixture of antiques and more modern furnishings.

Still, everything was pulled together in a way that was comfortable yet more upscale than expected for the age of the original building. The dining room had a long mahogany table in the center, with several smaller mahogany tables near the front windows. The serving buffet had a Marble top, and heating and cooling units. Underneath storage had been custom designed, yet the entire piece looked like a fifty-year-old antique.

After adding fresh tablecloths and linens to the tables, it struck Trish she hadn't yet seen Cassidy, but with a short amount of time left to get her work done, she decided to wait until she was finished to go looking for her.

Trish opened the large cabinet where they stored the better china and silverware and started moving stacks of plates and utensils to the buffet table. The work was easy, and it let her mind wander.

The first topic that pushed its way into her thoughts was Derrick. It had been several days since Trish had seen him, and she wondered if he might be avoiding her after the issues with the false alarms and her complaints about the parking tickets. She realized she was conflicted in her feelings about him. Her mind told her to avoid him, or there could be trouble. She should leave the past in the past and not carry over old feelings to the present. Yet, her heart told her she wanted to be around him more. She was confused.

The other item that had her a bit worried was Sarah and Tom. While the two had been thrown together because of the rewiring project, Sarah confided to Trish that she also had mixed feelings about Tom. On the one hand, he infuriated her, but on the other, she was drawn to him in a way that she hadn't been toward anyone else in years.

Then there was the issue of customers complaining about parking tickets, which seemed to be increasing, especially as the summer temperatures had started to soar. Cassidy was also complaining about the unusually early hot summer days and the need to turn on their sprinkler system at the inn, which drove up the water bill. Unlike other parts of the country, Maine typically had pleasant temperatures in early summer, which was one of the reasons they enjoyed a healthy vacation and tourism trade. This year was already warmer than usual, so residents and business owners didn't need parking ticket fines added to their air conditioning and water bills.

Trish was thinking about the hotter temperatures when she saw Cassidy enter the dining room.

"Well, it's about time you got here," Trish said. "I was getting ready to call you to see if you were okay. You're typically here at the crack of dawn. What's up?" As soon as Trish said it, she could see Cassidy's face was flushed, and she was slightly shaking.

Trish went to Cassidy, helped her friend get to a chair, and poured her a cold glass of water, "Oh my, what's wrong?"

Cassidy took a couple sips of the cool water. "I don't know. I got up this morning and had a slight headache, so I hung around the house for a while. Once I started feeling better, I decided some fresh air and a brisk walk were what I needed. But, about halfway here, the heat seemed to get to me, and I got sweaty and suddenly exhausted."

Cassidy's color was returning to its normal shade. "I feel fine now. I'm not used to the hot weather this early in the summer, and walking in the sun added to it. But I'm fine, so stop hovering."

Trish took a long look at her friend and agreed she looked much better, but something was off. She'd never seen

Cassidy overcome by a hot day. If Cassidy's husband, Jack, were home, she'd give him a quick call to come to the inn, but unfortunately, he was out of town on a book tour.

His international spy novels continued to grow in popularity, and Jack was routinely out of town, but that was the deal he'd made with his publisher and friend, Thornton Reed. Jack and Cassidy could continue to live in Lakeview, but Jack had to agree he'd be in New York City at the Patterson Publishing offices or on book tours as often as Thornton needed him. So far, it worked fine for all parties involved, but Trish wished Jack was only five minutes down the road on days like today.

The sound of Amanda and Peter entering the room prompted Cassidy to grab Trish's hand and whisper to her not to say anything about what had happened. Not sure what to do, Trish agreed to keep this between them for now, but they would discuss it later.

Guests started coming into the room as the final touches were put on the buffet, and Amanda and Trish greeted guests and kept the coffee flowing. Unfortunately, the four friends were kept extremely busy for the next three hours and had no time to chat, but they could hear bits and pieces of the conversation flowing around the dining room.

Yet again, the primary topic of discussion was 'time-expired' and the Town Council meeting, and today, another theme was added—odd happenings at Crystal Lake Gifts. Trish wasn't sure if she felt good about the word-of-mouth publicity or was discouraged the discussion was geared toward odd happenings and not the quality and variety of her merchandise.

As soon as the last guest left the dining room, Peter joined the three women as they filled their plates and finally sat down to eat their meal.

Trish was the first to speak. "I can't believe the buzz today about the drama from the Town Council meeting regarding the parking meter issues and the odd happenings at my shop. Typically, the conversation at the Sunday Brunch is more geared toward what our guests have been doing on their vacation, the weather, and the delicious food. I also can't believe someone would prefer to discuss parking meters versus Peter's tasty meal. What's gotten into everyone?"

"I've been upstaged by a parking meter," Peter said laughingly. "That's a first. Maybe next week we'll place parking meters in our parking lot. What do you think, Cassidy?"

Three sets of eyes looked toward Cassidy, who seemed oblivious that Peter had asked her a question. Instead, she appeared to be deep in thought about something else. Realizing everyone was staring at her, she quickly said, "Sorry. I was lost in thought. What did you ask me?"

Peter repeated his comments, and the group laughed, indicating all four thought it was a silly idea that didn't need a response.

Trish kept her eyes on Cassidy, concerned about her friend's distracted demeanor. *Should I call Jack? If I do, Cassidy will be so mad at me, and I promised to keep it to myself. I don't know what to do.*

CHAPTER TWELVE

Sunday was the busiest weekend day at the Lakeview Artisan community market, located a few miles from Main Street in the Pineview Mountains. It was all hands on-deck to ensure enough merchandise was made to not only keep the Crystal Lake store stocked but to sell to market customers as well. Several food trucks, ice cream vendors, and face-painting stands were on hand to make the day more enjoyable for everyone.

Walking tours of the various trades and art forms were also a big hit with the crowd, and Sarah routinely helped with the thirty-minute jaunts around the extensive grounds. Because the electrical job at Crystal Lake Gifts was on hold until Monday, when the next city inspection was scheduled, Sarah spent the day helping the artisans' team.

Many artisans made their products onsite, and customers could watch the process. Sarah loved to share their historical and handcrafted skills, especially with the younger audience, who typically seemed to be in awe of the timeless techniques.

After finishing a tour, Sarah stopped for a glass of homemade lemonade and was on her way to the small building they used for an office when she noticed a familiar face in the crowd. She was surprised to see Tom Spencer at a stall selling handmade aprons, hair bows, and baby doll clothes. As she got closer to the booth where Tom was standing, she noticed he was helping an adorable little girl, about five years old, pick out hairbows. Sarah thought how sweet it was for Tom to help someone's little girl until she noticed he was paying for the merchandise, and the little girl reached up and kissed Tom on the cheek. She took his hand as they continued to walk through the stalls.

Until now, Sarah assumed Tom was single. If he was divorced, he might have thought to mention it while they had been working so closely multiple evenings. Either way, it looked like Tom was doing 'daddy duty,' so she quickly sidestepped Tom and headed in the other direction.

Walking into the office, Sarah closed her door and sat behind her desk. *My life is complicated and hectic enough as it is. The fact that he wasn't entirely truthful with me hurts. What else is he hiding?* But, thinking about it further, Sarah gave Tom credit for being a good dad and exposing his daughter to the wholesome atmosphere of their little artisan village.

It hit Sarah like a lightning bolt. She'd love to have a little girl to make adorable dresses for, put bows in her hair, and cuddle with at bedtime, but she wasn't sure she was ready for an instant family. When she did have children, she wanted to be the primary mother and a full-time wife. She reminded herself again to steer clear of Mr. Spencer as much as possible.

Sunday afternoons were a restful time at the inn. Most guests checked in on Friday and Saturday, leaving Sunday afternoon for the staff to attend to personal chores or relax by the lake.

While staying at the inn, Trish insisted on doing her own laundry and cleaning her room. Once she completed her chores, she grabbed Jack's newest spy novel, released earlier in the week, and headed to the lake. After taking a leisurely walk down to the small waterfall about a mile from the inn, she returned to sit on one of the benches at the foot of the inn's meticulously manicured flowerbeds. She read several chapters of Jack's book before the light faded, making it difficult to see the words on the pages.

Looking out at the lake, Trish took a deep breath and immediately recognized the sweet floral smell of baby rose bushes and the aromatic scent of a large bed of purple petunias. If you sat in this exact spot as the evening rolled in, the purple petunia plants released an even sweeter-smelling fragrance with a subtle hint of cloves that attracted insects and pollinators.

As the sun started its slow descent, the sky showed a gradual color change, and the various flowers put on a kaleidoscope show of color. The combination often left visitors breathless. It reminded Trish that the scene before her was one not everybody across the country got to enjoy, and she was again thankful she lived in such a beautiful place surrounded by friends who were her chosen family.

Trish was so entrenched in enjoying the view she was startled when someone touched her shoulder. She looked up to see Jack standing next to her bench.

"Jack, you shouldn't sneak up on people. I dropped my book, or more accurately, your book," Trish said breathlessly.

"I hope you're enjoying the book," Jack responded with a big smile. He motioned for Trish to move over so he could join her on the bench.

"I didn't think you were due home until mid-week."

"There was a scheduling conflict at one of the bookstores on my itinerary, so the event was moved to later this week. That allowed me to come home for two days, which is great. But, on the other hand, I have to leave again and be gone for another week. It's a good thing I love what I do."

Jack stopped talking while he took in the stunning view of the sun as it continued its journey down the horizon and added touches of coral and indigo to the color wheel. Finally, Jack turned to face Trish, "This is one of the special moments I miss most when I travel. I also miss my wife and those famous chocolate chip cookies she makes for the evening Sit-n-Sip. Are you joining us on the porch this evening? If so, we need to get moving. We're already late."

Trish and Jack remained quiet as they walked toward the inn to join others who had already taken a seat on one of the porch swings or the numerous rockers. The nightly Sit-n-Sip was a favorite among the guests. It was a way to unwind, meet other guests, share stories of sightseeing adventures, or relax. It crossed Trish's mind she should mention the earlier situation with Cassidy, but she had promised to keep Cassidy's special secret.

Going inside the inn to see if she could help with anything, Trish saw that Cassidy looked fine but decided to keep a close eye on her best friend. "Can I help with anything?" Trish asked.

Amanda had the trolley used for the nightly event and was headed toward the porch. "Nope, we've got it covered, but please come out and join us. Even though you're staying at the inn, we never get to catch up with each other."

After the guests were served, Jack and Cassidy picked the swing at the end of the long porch while Peter, Amanda, and Trish pulled rockers closer together so the group could easily chat.

Jack was curious about what had been happening at the inn and in town while he'd been away and asked the group to share updates with him. Everyone started talking at once, and several times, people talked over each other and laughed. Everyone shared a funny story about the 'time-expired' parking meter saga and the odd happenings at Crystal Lake Gifts.

Trish leaned closer to Jack and confided she was concerned about what everyone called the odd happenings at Crystal Lake Gifts. "Jack, since you write about mysteries and create inventive and intriguing stories, do you have any suggestions on how to solve the mysteries at my shop?"

"I'm not a detective or investigator, but I could stop by and take a look around. How about tomorrow right after you open?"

"That would be wonderful. I'm looking forward to getting your input. I'll see you around ten o'clock in the morning."

Jack arrived at Crystal Lake Gifts promptly at ten the next morning, as promised, and headed straight for the office on the second floor. "Trish, are you up here?"

"Just a second, I'm pulling some stock out of the second-floor storage room. I'll be right there."

Jack hurried over to help Trish, who was trying to juggle several cartons. They split the stack of boxes, walked over to the long worktable, and placed the boxes on top.

"Thanks for your help, Jack. I always try to carry way too much. I'm excited to get these new summer dresses on the racks downstairs. I think they'll be a solid seller, but I'm still a little nervous about my new clothing line. It's too new to tell how it will do throughout the summer. Let's head downstairs, and I'll show you the current security and camera setup."

For the next thirty minutes, Trish showed Jack the entire store setup, the security system, the panic alarm, and three cameras installed when the security system was implemented. She also shared the issues with the wiring, false alarms, and someone stealing food from the breakroom.

Jack was so quiet it prompted Trish to ask, "What do you think?"

"It seems like all the pieces you described should have provided us with an answer, but I don't see any obvious gaps. The odd happenings are random and not tied together, or that is how it feels at this point."

Jack was thoughtful for a moment. "I brought some additional surveillance cameras left over from the upgrade we did at the inn. These six cameras were still in good shape.

Currently, you only have those three external cameras, so I recommend adding two more to the outside, including one that shows a view up Main Street, and adding the other four in various places inside the store, including the breakroom. I can work with your electrician to install them if he's available before I return to my tour. What do you think?"

Trish hesitated before responding, "I like the idea of the extra cameras, especially the one looking up Main Street, since we also have the current parking meter issue. I'm not sure about putting cameras in the breakroom. I worry the staff will feel like I'm watching them and ensuring they don't take too many breaks. What do you think?"

Before Jack could respond, Sarah walked into the room and answered the question Trish had asked Jack. "I think the staff will support the extra cameras. We want to find out what's happening around here, and I think everyone will feel a bit safer with them, including the one in the breakroom."

"Okay, Jack, I agree with your recommendations and with Sarah's assessment of how the staff will feel. Before you install them, I'll meet with the employees to review why we are adding the cameras so no one has an issue or feels uncomfortable. We are a small team, and I'm so fortunate everyone gets along well and takes great pride in their jobs. So, let's do it."

Trish and Jack continued to speak for several minutes. Finally, Jack agreed to call Tom Spencer and coordinate an installation date, and then he left the shop.

CHAPTER THIRTEEN

Sarah offered to do an afternoon coffee and cookie run and walked across the street to The Perk. She placed her order, chatted with Amy for a few minutes, and moved over to the end of the counter so Amy could wait on a group of women who had walked into the shop, including the town gossip, Mrs. Lester.

As usual, Mrs. Lester was engaged in an animated conversation, which Sarah wasn't interested in hearing. But as she turned back toward the counter, she heard Mrs. Lester talking about someone named Leah Foster and her daughter and how the new electrician in town, Tom Spencer, spent a lot of time with them.

Mrs. Lester continued, "Leah is so beautiful and a wonderful mother to her daughter Ellie. I think Leah will be a great addition to our little town." Several women agreed with Mrs. Lester and offered to stop by the Foster's home with welcome gifts, casseroles, and desserts. Mrs. Lester added, "Being neighborly is what we do in small towns, so let's coordinate our activities. As a matter of fact, I invited Leah to join us today here at The Perk."

The comment stunned Sarah briefly, but she realized she shouldn't be surprised since she had seen Tom with the little girl a few days ago at the Farmers' Market. It stung to have her fears confirmed. She was not only disappointed, but she was also angry. Tears gathered in her eyes, but she couldn't help but move closer to the group of women, hoping to hear more of their conversation.

Before she heard anything else, Amy called her name to let her know her order was ready. She returned to the pick-up area and grabbed her order.

While her back was turned, she failed to notice a pretty young woman in her early thirties had walked into the shop. As Sarah turned around to leave, she saw Mrs. Lester had quickly pulled someone she didn't know into her circle of friends and introduced her as Leah Foster.

Hearing the name Leah, Sarah stopped mid-step and came close to dropping her order but quickly recovered. As she continued to walk toward the front door, she had to step around the group of women, and the young woman turned sideways to allow Sarah to pass.

It was everything she could do not to gasp. It became clear that Leah Foster was at least seven or eight months pregnant. Sarah was so shocked. It took all her focus to steady her hands and walk toward the door. She left the coffee shop as quickly as possible without calling attention to herself.

Sarah stopped on the sidewalk to calm down and gather her thoughts. The previously unshed tears now ran down her cheeks. Her mind was still reeling, but her heart was saying, *why would Tom flirt with me when his wife was ready to deliver baby number two? I'm so glad I found out before I became even more involved.* But she quickly realized her feelings had already gotten deeper than she intended. Now, she was devastated.

Sarah quickly walked back to Crystal Lake Gifts and quietly delivered the coffee to the breakroom without being noticed. She couldn't face anyone right now, so she took the easy way out and sent Trish a text saying that something had come up and that she needed to leave for the rest of the day.

Sarah got into her car as the tears streamed down her cheeks and fell onto her shirt. *How can I be so stupid? I'm so over all of this. I don't need to be made a fool of in front of the entire town. The next time I see Tom, I plan to tell him he should be ashamed of himself.* Finally, Sarah dried her tears and headed home, where she planned to attack an entire container of Rocky Road ice cream.

Since Tom hadn't been able to connect with Sarah at the Artisans' Community Sunday, he decided to stop by Crystal Lake Gifts and took the chance she was working at the shop. He told himself the purpose of his visit was to check that no more electrical incidents had happened. He wouldn't admit, even to himself, that he was there to see Sarah.

A few minutes after Tom arrived at the shop, he returned to his truck. Trish had told him Sarah left for the day.

Something urgent had come up at the Artisans' Community and she needed to leave early.

Feeling disappointed, Tom wondered if he missed his chance to form a closer relationship with Sarah when they were working alone at the shop in the evenings. Thinking back over the past several weeks, he realized Sarah had been increasingly friendly and even brought him coffee from The Perk several times. She often stopped what she was doing to spend a few minutes chatting with him as he worked on the electrical system. He'd loved how easy it was to make her laugh and how her beautiful emerald-green eyes shined when she smiled.

But a few days ago, something happened that changed everything, and he couldn't put his finger on exactly what. *Did I do something to offend her?* It seemed like Sarah was avoiding him. Reminiscing on their last few evenings at the shop, Tom couldn't think of anything he'd done to push her away. Instead, they'd seemed to be getting closer and closer. Now, Tom was confused. He needed to talk to Sarah and find out what was going on.

He was startled to realize his feelings for Sarah were growing deeper than he originally intended. His life was hectic right now. Taking over the established business was a lot to handle, and helping his sister and her family left him with very little personal time. If he had used his brain, he would have said now wasn't the right time to start a serious relationship. But when it came to Sarah, he wasn't thinking with his brain—his heart was taking the lead, and right now, it told him this was a relationship worth fighting for, and that was precisely what he intended to do.

CHAPTER FOURTEEN

Main Street shoppers saw an increase in the 'time-expired' tickets. Everyone seemed to be in an uproar over the situation, but no one was doing anything constructive about it. Last week alone, two customers from Crystal Lake Gifts had tickets waiting for them once they left the shop. To make matters worse, when Trish completed her weekly sales reports, she noticed a slight dip in sales. It was hard to pin it directly on the parking meter situation, but she was confident the tickets were behind the drop.

Seeing the impact on her sales, Trish felt compelled to take action. She left the shop in the capable hands of a part-time clerk and headed to Town Hall, where the Police Department was located.

Trish marched into Derrick's office, and without waiting for him to look up from what he was reading on his computer screen, she started speaking in an aggravated voice, "This 'time- expired' parking meter situation is out of control. My sales were down last week, and everyone is in a tailspin. We need to do something. I'm not sure what can be done, but we need your help figuring out our options." Trish finally stopped to take a deep breath.

Feeling herself calm down, she decided to change her tactic and be friendlier since she was finding it hard to be mad at Derrick. "Can you join me for coffee at The Perk? I'm buying."

Derrick's face lit up with a big smile. "Hi Trish, it's nice to see you too. Invitation accepted. Should we call it a date?"

Trish started to sputter. She hadn't meant her invitation to sound like a date. Or had she? "I only asked you to join me to discuss the ticket issue. This is not a date."

"I guess I have time to assist a damsel in distress. I'll drive since I'm on duty and need my car in case I get an urgent call."

"No need to drive me. I walked here. It's only a few blocks back to The Perk. What would people think if they saw me in your police car? That's an excellent way to get rumors started. Since you'll get there before me, grab us a table and tell Amy I'll take my usual drink."

She was nervous and didn't want to be in the close confines of a car with Derrick, even if it was only for five minutes. She headed out the door and down the hall before Derrick could grab his hat and car keys.

Derrick caught up with her outside the front door of Town Hall and opened the passenger door, waiting for her to get in. After hesitating for a second, she realized it was silly to refuse his offer of a ride, so Trish got into the car.

Even though the console separated them, Trish could feel the heat from Derrick's body, and she got a slight whiff of the woodsy cologne he wore. Her nerves were on edge, and she realized she was shaking. Trying to relax, she took several deep breaths and looked directly out the front windshield, fearing Derrick would see his impact on her if she looked over at him.

After only going a block, they had to stop for a red light, and Derrick was distracted by something coming across the police monitor on his dashboard. It gave Trish time to let her thoughts drift back to their high school days. Sitting at this same red light, Derrick had always leaned over and kissed her. She wondered if his kisses were still as sweet as they had been back then.

Once the light changed, Trish returned to her senses, but the memory shook her. Why was she thinking this way? She wasn't interested in Derrick, or was she? One thing was for sure, she was confused.

Five minutes later, they parked in front of The Perk, and Trish quickly got out of the car, not leaving Derrick time to open her door. Instead, she hurried into the café and walked to the counter. Fortunately, Derrick's phone rang, and he stayed outside to take the call.

Trish was relieved Derick was delayed coming inside. It gave her a few minutes to get herself together, get her coffee, and find a table. By the time he joined her, she was more composed.

Derrick stopped at the counter to get his coffee and headed to the table. Sitting down, he said, "Sorry about the interruptions, but I'm officially still on duty."

Deciding to take a direct approach, Trish blurted out her concerns about the parking meters and the numerous complaints from merchants and customers. It seemed clear the problem wasn't going away without someone getting to the bottom of the situation, and Trish knew she needed Derrick's help. She made a few suggestions, and they both spoke about potential options for digging deeper into the problem.

Derrick's training had helped him to hear and see when something happened that was out of the ordinary. He'd heard too many complaints about the 'time-expired' situation, and decided he couldn't let the pot simmer any longer.

He'd given it some thought even before Trish showed up at his office today. He decided it was time to share his potential plan, but his thought process was abruptly halted. Suddenly, as he sat across from Trish at their table in The Perk, Derrick heard raised voices, which alerted his police-senses. He looked around to see where the voices were coming from.

He heard Amy, the owner of The Perk, talking to a male customer who seemed agitated about something. The customer paid for forty-five minutes of parking in front of her store. He stopped at the local newspaper office to drop off something, quickly stopped at the bank to use the ATM, and returned to The Perk to get his coffee. When he returned to his car, he had a parking ticket, and not even twenty minutes had lapsed. Amy offered to give the customer his coffee for free to help calm him down. Once he got his coffee, he turned and saw Derrick sitting at the table. The angry customer paused as if he were going to say something to the officer, but instead, he moved on, shaking his head as he stormed out the door.

Amy approached Derrick, "You've got to do something about this mess. I'm not the only merchant hearing these stories. I know Trish also feels the impact, but the merchants up a few blocks have even more issues than us."

"I think we need to canvas several of the merchants and get a better feel for the situation." Derrick asked Trish if she'd join him, and off they went.

An hour later, they had a long list of unhappy merchants. In reviewing the list, they realized the stores with the most issues seemed to be on the northern end of Main Street, not on the southern end of the street where the Town Hall and Police Department were located. There might be fewer complaints coming from near the Police Station because most people wouldn't complain about getting a ticket for parking directly at the Police Department. That could be why it had taken so long to get the proper attention from the authorities, Derrick figured.

He agreed to return to his office and have someone pull a report on the number of tickets, where the cars were parked, and the most frequent time of day the tickets were issued. In addition, he was going to pull the video from the department's recently installed cameras.

He was frustrated that his non-date with Trish had been interrupted by the 'time-expired' issue. He walked Trish back to the sidewalk and waited to ensure she got safely across the street. Once Trish entered the shop, Derrick returned to his cruiser and headed toward the Police Department. His instincts told him something wasn't right. He could always feel it in his gut when something was wrong.

Right now, his gut was speaking loudly. And it wasn't because he was hungry. He needed to get to the bottom of this problem or risk a rocky road not only with Trish but with the rest of his constituents.

Sitting in her office at the Inn, Cassidy gazed out the window. However, she failed to see the beautiful gardens flowering with a rainbow of colors or the sun glistening off the lake. She continued to stare, lost in her thoughts.

"Cassidy, I called your cell phone twice, and when you didn't answer, I decided to come and see if you were okay. When I walked into your office, you were staring out the window and didn't hear me come in. What's up?" Amanda asked with a look of concern on her face.

It took Cassidy another minute to pull herself together, "Nothing. Jack is due home tomorrow night, and I was thinking about planning a romantic dinner for the two of us. He's been gone over a week, and after eating out every night, he'll be craving a homecooked meal, and I'm craving a quiet evening at home with my hubby."

"If you're sure everything is okay. I'll leave it at that." Amanda started to walk away, but stopped abruptly, "Oh, I remembered why I called you in the first place. Since the Inn is quiet today, and Trish mentioned they were busier than usual at the shop and she needed to run a few errands, she hoped one of us could help for a few hours.

"I mentioned to Peter that I thought I'd go into town and help at Crystal Lake Gifts for a few hours, and he suggested maybe you'd want to go since you've been in your office for the past two days. I'm happy to go, or would you like to go? Either way is fine with me."

Cassidy looked at the clock on the wall and realized it was eleven o'clock. She had been in her office the entire morning and most of the previous day. "Peter is right. I need to get out of here for a few hours. I'll let Trish know I'm coming to help. I'll offer to stay until closing, but I think I'll go home after that, clean the house, and get the laundry done before Jack arrives tomorrow. I'll pass on dinner with you tonight but thanks."

"You look a bit pale, or maybe, as you say, you need to get outside in the sunshine. If you're sure everything is okay, go ahead and get moving. I need to get back to the front desk," Amanda said with a brief wave, walking back down the hall.

Not wanting Amanda to return and ask more questions, Cassidy grabbed her purse and headed to the back entrance, where the staff parked their cars. She got into her car and headed toward town, but halfway to Crystal Lake Gifts, she pulled over and parked her car in the outer parking spaces of the local library. She needed time to compose herself and add a little blush to her cheeks before entering the shop where Trish would see how pale she looked. Her two best friends knew her way too well, and if Trish looked closely at Cassidy in her current state, she wouldn't be able to brush off that nothing was wrong.

Getting her lipstick and blush out of her purse, she pulled down the car's visor and started to repair her makeup.

Suddenly, it all flooded her memory, and she returned to the scene in her doctor's office and the conversation she'd had with her doctor two days ago.

"Cassidy, I'm glad you agreed to get blood work done last week," Dr. Meade said as he closed the folder in front of him. "After your complete exam and looking at the blood work, I think I know exactly what is wrong with you."

"Oh my, I thought maybe I was overdoing it. Is there something seriously wrong with me? What can I do to fix whatever is wrong?" Cassidy had quickly blurted out. She'd realized her hands were shaking slightly.

"Cassidy, I've known you most of your life, and this is one diagnosis I'm happy to be able to share with you. Your little medical situation will resolve itself in about seven more months. I'm not sure if you and Jack were planning to start your family right now, but surprise, you're pregnant. I hope this is good news for you," Dr. Meade waited to see recognition of what he had told Cassidy to register on her face.

"I'm what? Pregnant? Are you sure?" Cassidy was trying to focus. Did the doctor tell her she was pregnant? Did she hear him correctly?

"Yes, I'm sure. The blood panel was done twice. Congratulations!"

Here are some pamphlets for you to read, some websites I recommend you review, and a prescription for prenatal vitamins. Also, you'll need to cut back on your schedule. I know from talking with your mother at our last hospital board meeting you still work sixty hours or more per week. I'd like you to reduce that to no more than forty hours per week for now and even less as you get closer to your delivery date. Also, keep up with daily exercise, reduce your sweets, and eat healthy meals."

Cassidy's thoughts whirled. "Once I can think straight, I'll figure out how to do everything you asked. Jack is out of town until tomorrow evening. I can't wait to share this news with him. And yes. it is good news. Maybe it's a bit sooner than planned, but it's what we wanted. I know you won't share this news with anyone, but once I tell Jack, he may shout it so loudly everyone in Lakeview will know."

The loud laughs of two children walking with their mother toward the library caught Cassidy's attention and brought her back to the present. Taking a deep breath to help calm her nerves, Cassidy fixed her makeup, flipped the visor back, and headed out of the parking lot. She was calmer and excited to share the news with Jack. But Trish needed her help at the shop, so she headed to Crystal Lake Gifts. Life was about to get interesting for her and Jack.

Two hours later, Cassidy was organizing new jewelry pieces in the antique glass case at Crystal Lake Gifts when she saw

Peter walking toward her. "Hello, Peter. This is a surprise. I didn't expect to see you here today. What's up?"

Peter walked over to Cassidy, putting his finger in front of his lips to signify he was about to tell her a secret. Keeping his voice low, he asked Cassidy to help him pick out a special birthday gift for Amanda. They walked around the entire shop without Peter finding what he was looking for, and as they stopped back at the jewelry counter, something caught Peter's eye.

"Please show me the birthstone ring sitting on the bed of dark blue velvet."

Cassidy opened the back door of the case, pulled out the velvet box, and placed it on top of the counter. She stood back, allowing Peter to admire the ring—a ruby set in a handmade golden rose setting. "The creation is one-of-a-kind and gorgeous. It will look fantastic on Amanda's finger. I'll give you a few minutes to consider your purchase and come back and check on you."

Cassidy walked away from the counter to give Peter some private time, but as she walked away, she wondered if the ring was a birthday gift or the promise of something deeper between Peter and Amanda. Those two were close, spent most of their time together, and clearly, they were in love. Cassidy and Trish had both recently remarked on the question of potential wedding bells in the near future.

Cassidy returned to the jewelry counter and asked Peter, "What do you think?"

"It's perfect. I'll take it. Can you gift wrap it for me, please?"

Cassidy wrapped the gift in beautiful floral paper and added a small bow to the top before putting the box into a gift bag. "Here you go. I know Amanda will love it."

"Please keep this a secret. I want to give it to her at a romantic dinner I'm cooking on my sailboat. I'm going all out with her favorite food, wine, dessert, and candles. She works so hard, and it's been hectic lately, so I want it to be a special evening."

"Of course. I won't say a word to anyone. Your secret is safe with me."

CHAPTER FIFTEEN

Peter lingered in the store after Cassidy handed him his gift bag. "While I'm here, I want to speak with Sarah for a minute about ordering additional aprons for the kitchen and serving staff at the inn," he said. "Some of ours have stains that won't come out. We love the way she embroiders them with the inn's logo, but we seem to be a bit messy." Peter chuckled as he walked away from Cassidy and headed toward the other side of the shop where the handmade goods were displayed, and Sarah was restocking shelves.

Ten minutes later, Sarah finished writing the special embroidering order for Peter and walked with him to the front of the shop. Peter got a call from one of his suppliers and excused himself to take the call. Sarah indicated he could take the call from their breakroom down the hall.

Sarah heard the bell ring over the front door and noticed a well-dressed man entering the shop. She'd never seen the person in the shop before, and he seemed a bit lost. Sarah approached him and asked if she could help. He hesitated for a minute, pulled a hairbow from his pocket, and explained his daughter loved the handmade bows she got at the Artisans' Market a few weeks earlier but lost the match to the one in his hand. He heard Crystal Lake Gifts sold handmade items and had hoped to find something similar.

"You've come to the right place. Our local artisan group sells similar items here in the shop. I think I have the match to the hairbow in your hand." Sarah took a few steps to a display and picked two to show the gentleman. "Fortunately, we have two more sets exactly like the one you showed me. This light pink set is close to the one you brought into the store, and we also have a set in white. Would you like the pink set?"

"Yes, I'll take it, and I'll also take the white set. My daughter will be thrilled. You've saved me from running all over town or going home to my five-year-old daughter's pouting face."

"Here you go. You can take the items to the front counter, and Cassidy will ring up your sale. Thanks for supporting our local artisans."

The man browsed through several aisles and headed to the front counter. Cassidy asked if the customer had found everything he was looking for, finished the sale, and put the bows in a bag.

As Cassidy reached for the receipt to give to the customer, the numbers on the register suddenly danced around before her eyes and turned blurry. She was lightheaded and tried to grab the counter to steady herself, but instead, she felt her body going limp. The last thing she clearly remembered was knocking the stapler off the counter and someone grabbing her under her arms to stop her fall.

Peter and Sarah heard the clatter of something hitting the floor. When they turned around, they saw a man helping to ease Cassidy into a chair. She seemed limp, with her head rolled forward onto her chest. Peter and Sarah ran over to where the man was sitting Cassidy in a chair, his arms holding her in place.

In the few seconds it took for Peter and Sarah to reach the counter, they noticed Cassidy seemed to be coming around. Her eyes were fluttering, but she was still pale, shaking, and still a bit incoherent.

"Cassidy, are you all right? What happened?" Sarah and Peter ask simultaneously.

Without turning away from Cassidy, the man called out, "Please dial 911 and ask them to send the EMTs. Tell the dispatcher a woman in her early thirties passed out, has an elevated pulse, and her color is pale."

The stranger's commanding tone left no room for argument. Sarah pulled her cell phone from her pocket, dialed 911, repeated what the stranger had said to the dispatcher, and gave the address of the shop—Crystal Lake Gifts, located at 300 Main Street, directly across from The Perk. Please hurry."

As soon as Sarah hung up, she turned to the stranger to ask who he was, but he spoke first, "I'm Dr. Sam Foster, a member of the senior medical team at Lakeview Hospital. Do you know this woman?"

After getting a positive response from Sarah, he continued his questions, "Are you aware of any reason why she might have passed out? Does she have diabetes or another serious medical condition?"

When Sarah and Peter both said no, Dr. Foster said, "Please let me have a minute with this young lady before the paramedics arrive. Can you keep the other customers away from this area? I want to give her a little privacy. Did I hear you call her Cassidy?"

Sarah nodded yes, and she and Peter moved away from the area. They kept other shoppers back, telling them the man at the counter was a doctor. Sarah briefly took one last look at her friend. As she started to turn around, she noticed Cassidy's eyes had fluttered open, and some color had returned to her face. Hopefully, she was recovering from whatever had happened.

The man still held Cassidy's hand and spoke calmly to her, "My name is Dr. Sam Foster. Can I call you Cassidy? I'm a Neonatal Specialist from Lakeview Hospital. I want to take your pulse. Is that okay with you?"

Cassidy was still shaky and scared, but the fuzziness was starting to lift.

She motioned for Dr. Foster to lean closer. "It's okay to call me Cassidy, and yes, it's fine for you to take my pulse."

There seemed to be some recognition click for Cassidy. In her nervousness, her mind was running in circles, but the first thing she said was, "I think I met you before—maybe at the big gala for the new Neonatal Unit last year."

Dr. Foster put his finger in front of his lips, indicating Cassidy should be quiet for a minute. Then, surprisingly, or maybe not for a doctor, he pulled a stethoscope out of his suit jacket pocket and checked Cassidy's heart. Once he was done, he asked her if she knew of any reason why she'd be lightheaded and have a fast pulse.

Trying to clear her head and focus on the question, Cassidy took a few seconds to respond. Keeping her voice barely above a whisper, "I found out yesterday I'm pregnant. It's my first pregnancy. I haven't told anyone yet. My husband is out of town on business, and I want to share the news with him first."

Dr. Foster rechecked her pulse and asked Cassidy to stand up slowly, but she was still a bit shaky, so the doctor asked her to sit back in the chair until the EMTs arrived. "Your pulse is still a bit faster than I like. Have you had lunch? Did you drink plenty of fluids today?"

Cassidy looked embarrassed and admitted she had not eaten lunch but had taken in plenty of fluids.

"While these symptoms might be normal, to be on the safe side, I recommend letting the paramedics take you to the Emergency Room. I'll contact your doctor and ask him to meet us there. I'll follow in my car and stay with you until your OBGYN arrives." Dr. Foster pulled out his cell phone. "Cassidy, don't worry. These symptoms happen all the time in the first trimester of pregnancy. After that, you should be fine with the proper rest, nutrition, and exercise. Fortunately for you, Lakeview Hospital has a world-class Neonatal Unit. I should know. I head it up." He gave her a big grin.

To help keep Cassidy occupied until the EMTs arrived, Dr. Foster told her how he came to be in Lakeview. The Board of the Lakeview Hospital made him an offer he couldn't refuse, so he left a much larger hospital on the West Coast and relocated to Lakeview a few months ago. "Once I saw what a wonderful and family-friendly place Lakeview was, I sent for my wife and daughter. They recently joined me here in your peaceful town. My wife, Leah, and our five-year-old daughter, Ellie, love it here, although, with my schedule, I don't have as much time to spend with them as I'd like. We're expecting our second child in two months, so my brother-in-law has been helping. I think you might know him. Tom owns Lakeview Electrical Services and mentioned he's been working for the shop owner."

Looking out the window, Dr. Foster announced, "The ambulance is here. Let's get you on the stretcher and to the ER."

With the patient securely strapped in, the stretcher headed toward the door, but Cassidy asked the EMT to stop so she could speak with her friends. She wasn't sure how much of her conversation with Dr. Foster they had overheard, and they still looked concerned.

As soon as the stretcher came to a stop, Sarah reached down and hugged Cassidy, and it was clear from the big smile on her face Sarah had heard she was pregnant. "Please don't mention this to anyone, including Jack," Cassidy pleaded. "I want to share this news with him when he gets home tomorrow evening. If anyone asks, I had a dizzy spell, and Dr. Foster suggested I go to the ER as a safety precaution. Please don't worry. I'm already feeling much better."

After a quick discussion, it was decided Sarah would call Trish and let her know what happened, but only about the dizzy spell. Sarah would stay at the shop. Peter would call Jack, who had already secretly planned to come home a day earlier than expected to surprise Cassidy. Hopefully, he was nearing Lakeview. Next, he would call Amanda and tell her about the dizzy spell before she heard it through the grapevine. It was good Amanda knew Peter was stopping by the shop to re-order aprons. Now, he would be keeping two secrets—Cassidy's pregnancy and the ring he purchased for Amanda.

Sarah followed the EMTs to the sidewalk and hugged Cassidy again before they loaded her into the back of the ambulance. Before the ambulance doors shut, Sarah said, "Don't worry, Cassidy. Everything will be fine."

Once inside the store, Sarah was still shaking, so she headed to the breakroom and grabbed a calming cup of herbal tea. She replayed the scene in her head and was thankful the new doctor from Lakeview Hospital was in the shop when Cassidy had her dizzy spell. She'd have been terrified if Cassidy had passed out and no one was there to help. Dr. Foster seemed like an excellent doctor, and it was great how he kept a running conversation going with Cassidy to help keep her calm until the EMTs arrived.

As Sarah finished her tea and walked to the sink to wash her mug, she stopped dead in her tracks. It was like a thousand-watt bulb went off in her head, and she started putting pieces together. She realized Dr. Foster said his brother-in-law's name was Tom. He owned Lakeview Electrical and spent a lot of time helping out with his little girl, who loved hairbows.

Was Dr. Foster talking about Tom Spencer? Could it be the little girl and pregnant woman Sarah mistakenly thought were Tom's wife and daughter were his sister and niece?

What a fool she'd been to let her imagination run wild. She had been so unfair not to speak to Tom about her concerns. A simple conversation could have sorted out this entire misunderstanding, and she wouldn't have wasted the past few weeks avoiding him.

I feel so stupid, and I owe Tom an apology.

She continued to berate herself for being so short-sighted and jumping to conclusions. Maybe she should call him, but quickly rejected that idea. She needed to see him in person and explain the situation while also asking for forgiveness.

Sarah finally admitted to herself that something was brewing between her and Tom. She needed to see if he would forgive her or if her recent lack of trust in him was a deal breaker. She realized Tom could walk away and not want anything further to do with her.

It made her anxious to think Tom might not forgive her. Somehow, Tom had worked his way into her heart over the past few weeks. She needed to explain her behavior, hoping he would forgive her. There had to be a way to see where this 'electricity' between them might lead.

CHAPTER SIXTEEN

Trish looked down at her wrist to check the time on her watch and was shocked to see two hours had passed since she and Derrick entered The Perk. At first, their conversation focused solely on the parking ticket debacle, but it turned to odd happenings at Crystal Lake Gifts, which became an update on the shop's rewiring project.

Suddenly, Derrick's hand-held police radio made a high-pitched screeching sound, alerting him to an emergency call. They both stopped talking so Derrick could hear the call.

The 911 dispatcher stated that EMTs and an ambulance were needed at 300 Main Street, along with police personnel, to manage Main Street traffic. The subject was Cassidy Taylor Burnett. Derrick responded by letting the dispatcher know he was two seconds away from the address and would take the lead for the emergency call.

As Derrick quickly exited his chair, he noticed Trish was still rooted in her seat and seemed shocked. He leaned down, touched her arm, pulled her to her feet, and said, "I've got to go now. Perhaps you should stay here until I assess the situation. I'm sure Cassidy is fine— maybe it's only a minor mishap." And with those words, Derrick ran out of The Perk and across the street.

Amy, the owner of The Perk, came over to Trish, touched her arm, and said, "Trish, did you hear the call on the police scanner? They mentioned they needed EMTs for someone, and I think I heard them say Cassidy's name. Do you want me to walk across the street with you? You seem to be in shock. Can I get you a glass of water?"

As if a volt of electricity had hit her, Trish started breathing again. In her haste to get to the shop, she knocked her chair over backwards getting to her feet, but didn't stop to pick it up. Since people had already spilled out of The Perk onto the sidewalk, Trish had to push through the crowd to get across the street.

She saw Derrick moving spectators out of the way, but she couldn't seem to get through the crowd. When she looked up again, she saw the stretcher was already coming out the door and down the shop's steps.

Trish loudly called Derrick's name, and he reached through the crowd and pulled her over to the ambulance doors, where the EMTs were headed with the stretcher.

Trish could see Cassidy was awake but looked pale, and it was clear she was scared.

"Trish, I'm fine," Cassidy said as they loaded her into the ambulance. "I had a dizzy spell, and fortunately, a doctor was in the shop. He insisted I go to the ER to be checked out as a precaution. Please don't worry. I'll be fine."

Before Trish could respond, the EMTs pushed the stretcher into place in the ambulance, where a loud click confirmed the patient was secured. There was a loud bang as the doors closed, and two seconds later, the vehicle was speeding down the street and headed toward Lakeview Hospital.

As the ambulance's taillights disappeared down the street, Derrick turned back to the crowd, asking them to disperse. Next, he checked with one of his officers on the scene to ask them to stay and take the reports.

Derrick needed to head to the hospital, but first, he turned around to find Trish. He could see she was upset and shaking. "Trish, the EMT said it was a dizzy spell. Cassidy will be fine. Jump in my cruiser if you want to go to the emergency room. I can get you there in a couple of minutes."

Derrick took Trish's arm, led her across the street to his car, and opened the front passenger door for her to get in the car. As he reached for her arm to help her get in, she broke down in tears. Without thinking, Derick put his arms around Trish to comfort her. It took a minute, but she calmed down and looked up into Derrick's eyes, and he continued to embrace her, letting her know he wanted to be there for her, to protect and comfort her, if only she'd let him.

The scene in the ER waiting room was chaotic. Stretchers were coming and going, EMTs and hospital staff moved with efficient actions behind curtains, and monitoring equipment beeped. About a dozen curtains were pulled around beds used for make-shift examination rooms with a nurses' station in the center.

It took Trish a second to scan the room. She headed to the nurses' station and waited for the young man in light blue scrubs to look up from his computer. "May I help you?" Trish noticed he looked exhausted, and it was clear he had run his hand through his hair several times. Trish silently wondered if he knew he had a pen behind both ears.

"The Lakeview EMTs brought in my friend, Cassidy Burnett. I need to see her."

"Her family is in the Waiting Room. Turn around and look to your left. You'll see the sign. Several people have already arrived in the past few minutes."

Trish started to ask the young man another question when the phone rang, and he turned his attention to the phone.

Walking across the room, she entered the waiting room. Trish looked for familiar faces. She immediately saw Amanda and Cassidy's mother, Kate. She assumed Peter had called them, and they must have arrived seconds before she had. As soon as Kate saw Trish, she pulled Trish and Amanda into a warm hug, which Trish appreciated.

Kate had always called Amanda and Trish her bonus daughters, and right now, Trish needed the comfort of her 'bonus mom.' As Kate stepped back from the hug, Trish saw the worried look on her face, but Trish also noticed the sense of calm Kate tried to extend to the two friends. Kate was a strong, determined woman who was always helpful in stressful situations.

Turning around to see who else was in the room, she noticed Peter was standing back from the group, but he didn't seem to have the same worried look as everyone else. Trish assumed it was a 'man thing' not to show his emotions, but she was shocked he could stay so calm when their best friend had been rushed to the hospital, and they had no idea what was happening.

Trish walked over to Peter and, keeping her voice low, said, "Peter, I heard you were in the shop when Cassidy had her dizzy spell. What happened?"

Hearing what Trish asked Peter, Amanda and Kate joined them. When Peter hesitated, Kate spoke up. "Yes, Peter, please tell us what happened to my daughter?"

Peter was now on the hot seat, but he had promised Cassidy not to share her secret. "By the time Sarah and I realized something was wrong, a man, identifying himself as Dr. Sam Foster, was helping Cassidy into a chair and taking her pulse. The Doctor pulled a stethoscope out of his suit jacket pocket and checked her heart. He said her pulse and heartbeat were faster than he liked and asked Sarah to call 911.

"It all happened so fast, and Cassidy seemed to be in good hands, so we stepped out of the way and let the Doctor control the situation. It only took two to three minutes for the EMTs to arrive, and then I jumped in my car to get to the ER and called you and Amanda."

"Well, being on the hospital Board of Trustees should have some privilege, so I'm going to the nurses' station and ask to see the doctor attending to my daughter," Kate said frowning. "And I don't plan to take 'no' for an answer."

Cassidy was in the room on the other side of the family waiting room, so she could hear everything her family and friends were saying. She could hear the worry in her mother's voice, and she looked at Dr. Foster, who had completed an internal exam and reported all to be well, along with the ultrasound that also looked good. He was reading something on her chart and seemed oblivious to what was happening next to her small room. "Dr. Foster, have you heard from my OBGYN yet?"

Dr. Foster looked up from the chart and smiled, "His service says he's in the hospital, but in a delivery right now. So, we shouldn't expect him for another thirty minutes. I put a rush on the blood work and hope to have it back any minute now. I've entered all my exam results into your electronic patient record and plan to stay with you until I hand you over to your OBGYN. Your vitals are much better, but it's important you relax."

"I know my mother and friends are worried. I can hear them drilling Peter about what happened, but I made him promise not to share my news. I want Jack to be the first to know. I've put Peter in a difficult situation. Maybe I should tell them the news, but on the other hand, would it be better to wait until the blood work returns and I can safely tell them everything is okay?" Cassidy shifted uncomfortably in the bed.

Dr. Foster reached for Cassidy's hand, "You need to do what's best to allow you to relax. But I can see you're still stressed. Maybe it's because you haven't been able to reach your husband yet, or you don't want to worry your family unnecessarily. Still, it's your decision to keep your medical condition to yourself or share your news. I can't tell you what to do, except if you plan to tell your family anyway, it might reduce the stress on everyone if you share something with them. At this point, I feel comfortable saying you'll be going home as soon as your OBGYN can do his exam and reinforces my instructions that you need to reduce your work schedule and get more rest."

Cassidy smiled and looked Dr. Foster straight in the eyes, "I'm also worried if my mother doesn't get answers soon, she'll start using her clout as a Lakeview Hospital Board member, creating unnecessary churn for everyone. My sweet and loving mother can become a bear when protecting her cubs. I should talk to her first. Would you mind getting her and asking her to come see me?"

Before Dr. Foster got the chance to leave the room, his phone beeped. "Your blood work report is ready. Let me review it on my iPad." He briefly scanned the screen and smiled. "Everything looks good, except your iron levels are a little lower than I'd like, but taking the prenatal vitamins should correct that in a few days. I'm happy to say, besides the low iron levels, you're a healthy expectant mother."

"Now that we can confirm your test results show everything is fine, I'll get your mother, and you can share your good news."

As Dr. Foster walked out of Cassidy's room to get her mother, he saw a tall and handsome man in a suit, minus the tie he clutched in his hand, approach Kate. He heard her call him Jack.

Before he could approach Jack, the doctor watched as he looked frantically from one friend to another, trying to determine what was happening. He finally saw Jack approach Kate. His hands are shaking, and his face is pale.

Dr. Foster knew it was time to help turn this situation around, but not before he let Cassidy share her news with Jack.

As soon as everyone noticed Dr. Foster had walked out of Cassidy's room, they immediately became silent. Finally, he stepped over to Jack, "Are you Cassidy's husband, Jack? She wants to see you first. She also asked me to tell everyone else she loves you and for you to sit down and stop worrying. She'll give you an update in a few minutes."

Dr. Foster led Jack into Cassidy's room. Jack took a second to process what he saw. Cassidy was in a hospital gown, lying on white sheets with an IV bag hanging from a pole and various equipment near her bed. The doctor could tell Jack thought the worst as he walked over to Cassidy, leaned down, and gently kissed her.

Jack quietly said to his wife, "Please tell me what is going on. I can handle the news, even if it's bad, but what I can't handle is not knowing what's wrong. I love you Cassidy, and your family and friends love you. Whatever it is, we can get through this together."

Cassidy broke out with a big smile and let out a little giggle, which caught Jack off guard, but he remained silent.

"Jack, I love you so much, but why did you immediately think I was seriously ill? Sweetheart, I'm fine. The doctor ran some tests and found my iron was low, which caused me to get lightheaded. Also, being eight weeks pregnant would make you a little dizzy. But Dr. Foster says the baby and I are doing fine."

Cassidy and Dr. Foster looked at Jack, who hadn't said a word and appeared whiter than the sheets on the bed.

"Jack, did you hear what I said? We're going to have a baby in about seven months." Cassidy stopped to give Jack time to process what she said.

When Jack still hadn't responded, Cassidy asked, "Jack, are you okay? Are you happy with the news? Maybe you should sit down. You look a little pale."

Dr. Foster pulled a chair beside the bed and pushed Jack into it. He didn't want to have to get a couple of orderlies to help him pick this tall man up off the floor.

Jack finally spoke. "Cassidy, can you repeat what you said? I think I misunderstood."

Cassidy repeated, "Jack, we're pregnant! We'll have a baby in about seven months. I hope you're as thrilled as I am, but I'm sure it's a bit of a surprise. You know my cycles are prone to get out of whack, so I didn't even think about it, and time moves so quickly it hadn't even crossed my mind."

Catching both Cassidy and Dr. Foster off guard, Jack let out a loud "WHOOP!" and ran over to kiss Cassidy. "Darling, I'm so happy but also a little bit confused. I got a call you were rushed to the hospital after collapsing, and of course, my mind went to the worst-case scenario. But I'm so happy about the baby. We planned to start our family soon, it just began sooner than expected. I couldn't be happier."

Dr. Foster added, "I heard from your OBGYN, who was on his way down to the ER to see you, but he received a request to help another doctor deliver twins. He took a few minutes to review your chart and test results, and he's fine with me releasing you to go home. Jack, he said to tell you congratulations.

"And Cassidy, he asked you to call his office in the morning to make a follow-up visit. It was nice getting to know you, Cassidy, but next time, I'd prefer it if it were under better circumstances, like dinner at your inn some Sunday. Several of my patients have raved about your food.

"I know you're anxious to get home, so I'll prepare your paperwork. A nurse will come in to go over the instructions and help get you ready to leave. I'm glad everything is going to be okay. Remember, reduce your work hours, take prenatal vitamins, drink plenty of fluids, and get extra rest. I'm sure Jack will happily wait on you for a few days. Also, don't return to work until you clear it with your OBGYN."

Forgetting the thin walls between her room and the waiting room, Cassidy didn't need to wait to tell her mother and friends the news. Five seconds after Jack's loud "whoop," Cassidy's room was filled with family, friends, smiles, and love.

CHAPTER SEVENTEEN

The past two weeks had flown by for Trish. Sales had been brisk at the shop, and the staff was kept busy serving customers, lifting heavy boxes, and restocking shelves. Every bone in her body cried out for a relaxing evening at the inn. She was thankful it was Saturday and the shop, like most retail stores in Lakeview, closed at five p.m.

Thinking back over the past week, she was relieved there hadn't been any issues with the burglar alarms or electrical problems. More importantly, Cassidy felt much better, and her OBGYN released her from bed rest. But, of course, Jack was still hoovering and acting like a mother hen.

Looking at her watch, Trish saw it was five p.m., so she walked to the front door and turned the sign to CLOSED. There were few people on the sidewalks except for activity around several restaurants.

Trish turned the lights off as she headed to the breakroom to get her purse. She looked around to ensure everything was in its place, set the alarm, and headed out the back door to the alley where her car was parked.

As she drove down Main Street, she passed the Lakeview Town Hall and couldn't help but look to see if Derrick's car was parked in his reserved spot. Yes, his car was in its usual spot, and she wondered if he had worked all weekend.

Thinking of Derrick reminded her of the hug they shared when Cassidy was rushed to the ER. She had to admit having someone to lean on during a crisis was comforting. And Derrick was the perfect person to rely on. He'd remained calm and in control during the entire emergency. She felt a blush coloring her cheeks when they hugged, and her heart rate quickened. Driving away from Main Street, her last thought was whether Derrick felt the same.

Driving out of town, Trish debated going back to speak with Derrick and thank him for being there for her and Cassidy. Of course, she could use the apology as a ploy, but what she really wanted to know was if Derrick would mention the special moment they shared. So far, their relationship had been strictly professional, but she wondered if he had also felt something stir in him or if it had just been wishful thinking on her part.

She wasn't sure of herself when it came to the Chief of Police, so she decided to head to the inn. The route took her less than two miles out of town. As she made the last turn in her journey, the lake came into view, and she automatically started to relax. She couldn't wait to change into more comfortable shoes and enjoy the rest of the evening.

With only half a mile to go, her mobile phone suddenly erupted with a loud alarm. It scared Trish, and she safely pulled off the road to see what was happening. Looking at her phone, she realized the alarm system at the shop had been tripped. She sat there momentarily and took a few deep breaths to calm her nerves. *Is it an intruder, or is it another fault with the system?* Since she couldn't tell from looking at the alarm app on her phone, she turned around and headed back into town.

Retracing her route took less than ten minutes. Then, as if they had planned it, Trish and Derrick arrived at the shop at the same time.

"Stay in your car with the doors locked and your windows up," Derrick yelled into her car window. "Look at the alarm app on your phone. Which door or window is tripping the alarm?"

Trish looked at the app and showed Derrick the phone through the window. "It's the front door."

"Stay put. I mean it. Do not open your car door until I come back outside." Derrick cautiously walked to the front door and wiggled the handle. The door was securely locked, so he returned to Trish's car. In a direct and stern voice, Derrick slowly said, "Turn the alarm off using your app."

Trish turned off the system. The alarm went silent, and the silence was blissful. She started to open her door, but Derrick told her to stay in the car until he did a walkthrough of the shop and checked the back door. He asked for the door key, returned to the front door, and unlocked it.

Trish saw Derrick walking through the front rooms, but he disappeared as he walked toward the back of the shop. She was nervous since she couldn't see him. Only a few minutes had passed, but it seemed like ten before she saw him again by the front door.

As Derrick returned to her car, she saw a deputy pull up behind her and get out. After a brief discussion, the deputy drove away and Derrick walked over to Trish and motioned for her to roll her window down.

"Trish, this is getting to be a big problem. The town has already fined you for not correcting the faulty alarm, and before you protest, I know you've had it worked on again, but something is still wrong. So, on Monday, you can expect another fine."

"What else can I do to stop these alarms? If I don't turn on the system, my insurance company will terminate my coverage. If I leave the system on, the town continues to fine me. I'm stuck in a no-win situation."

"Unfortunately, it looked like the power was out momentarily, sending another false alarm. The alarm should have a battery backup and when the power goes out or is cut, the battery takes over, and your alarm system continues to work. The message on the display panel says power failure."

The adrenaline had kicked in, and now Trish was struggling to relax. Derrick noticed she was still shaking, and he was concerned about letting her drive away. He made a snap decision, "The alarm came at the end of my shift, and I was headed to the Lakeview Diner to grab a bite. Would you care to join me?"

The invitation caught Trish off guard. She hesitated before responding as she wasn't clear if this was a date or a pity invite. "I haven't had dinner either, so yes, I'd like to join you. I'll drive the few blocks to the diner and after dinner, I can leave from there to return to the inn. I'll join you at the diner in a minute. I need to make two phone calls first. I need to let Sarah know everything is okay, and I want to ask Tom Spencer to stop by tomorrow to see if he can identify the issue."

After Derrick returned to his police car and drove off, Trish sat in her car and replayed the scene in her head. Derrick was all business one minute, yet he invited her to dinner the next. It was confusing, and she couldn't tell if something was brewing between them or not.

Trish pulled down the visor, looked in the mirror, and noticed she looked pale and had messy hair. She repaired her makeup, added a swipe of lip gloss, and combed her hair. While still slightly shaking, her color had started to return. Deciding she had better get going, or Derrick might think she'd changed her mind, she quickly flipped the visor back into place and started her car.

After the short drive, Trish arrived at the diner. Since it was still light outside, she noticed the flowers in the hanging baskets were more luscious than last week. As the sun lowered in the sky, it created a backdrop behind the baskets. The overall effect was stunning. The scene had a calming effect on Trish, and she hoped it would help her to face a meal in a confined space with Derrick.

Trish walked into the diner and saw Derrick sitting in one of the booths along the windows overlooking Main Street. It was a table visible to anyone who entered the front door, and whoever sat there could easily be noticed by those passing by and the other patrons in the restaurant. She preferred a table in the back, which was more private.

Derrick looked up as Trish approached the table. He slid out of the booth to help Trish slide across from him. He also took the shawl she grabbed from the car at the last minute, in case the restaurant was chilly, and carefully folded it over the back of her seat. Trish was surprised he was such a gentleman.

The server was new. Her name tag said her name was Claire. "What can I get you two to drink?" They settled on a bottle of sparkling water for now. "I'll be right back to take your orders."

Derrick and Trish started to speak at the same time and then stopped talking. "Derrick, you go first.".

"No, you go first, Trish. What did you start to say?"

She took a deep breath to calm her nerves, "I wanted to thank you for responding to the alarm at my shop and making sure everything was okay. And thanks for understanding how frustrating the situation has been. On the one hand, I couldn't be happier about how the renovations turned out, and while the business is exceeding our original projections, recently, we've seen a slight dip in sales. On the other hand, between the electrical issues, the alarm malfunctions, and now the parking meter issues, I feel like I'm constantly in an undertow and being sucked beneath the water. I shudder to think what might be next, although I'm afraid to say that out loud."

She saw an empathic look on Derrick's face, which made her stop talking. She took a deep breath and tried to relax.

The server returned, took their orders, and left a basket of warm dinner rolls and soft butter on the table. The smell of the fresh rolls caused Trish's stomach to rumble. Both Trish and Derrick reached for a roll at the same time, and their hands touched. Trish felt a slight tingle and looked up. Did Derrick also feel it? He had a good poker face, and she couldn't tell what he was thinking.

"Derrick, what were you going to say when I interrupted you?"

Derrick put down his roll and gazed into Trish's eyes, "I'm happy to be able to help you. I know multiple things are going on, which can cause extra stress. We'll figure out the parking meter issues. Let's change the topic to more pleasant conversation and enjoy our meals."

Their meals arrived, and before she realized it, two hours had passed.

"Derrick, I didn't mean to take up your entire evening. Thank you for the invitation. I hadn't had the diner's pot roast in months. It's always tender and delicious, but I'm stuffed. I think I'll head back to the inn and take a leisurely walk around the lake. Let me split the bill with you." Trish reached into her purse and pulled out her wallet.

"Absolutely not. I invited you to dinner, and it's my treat." After hesitating, Derrick casually added, "How do you feel about me joining you for a walk around the lake? I could use the exercise, and the sunset will be gorgeous tonight."

Trish was surprised when Derrick asked to extend their evening. She wanted to say yes, but would she regret it later? After a slight pause, she quietly said, "I'd like that."

They got up from the table, and Derrick grabbed Trish's shawl and held it for her to pull around her shoulders. He lightly touched her back and guided her to the door. He stepped aside, allowing her to walk through the door first. Once they reached the sidewalk, Derrick's hand returned to her back.

Her heart started to beat a bit faster, and she wasn't sure why. Was she still overly anxious from the earlier false alarm, or was being this close to Derrick causing her to experience feelings she hadn't in years? Her mind was going in circles.

When they got to their cars, Derrick reached around her to open the door and waited for her to get behind the wheel. Before he closed the door, he lightly touched her arm and said he'd meet her at the inn.

Goosebumps trickled up her arm, and she felt like a teenager. She needed to pull herself together. With that thought, Trish took a deep breath and drove to the inn.

Since they arrived at the same time, Trish told Derrick she needed to run to her room and change into more casual clothes and walking shoes.

Once in her room, Trish sat on the comfy chair near the window. She was reasonably sure the butterflies in her stomach were not due to the amount of food she ate at dinner. *I wonder if Derrick felt the electricity between us, or was it just me?*

She was wasting time and needed to get moving. She walked over to the dressing table, quickly applied lip gloss, fluffed her hair, and rushed outside.

Trish found Derrick on the walkway to the lake and joined him.

As she looked across the lake, the sky immediately grabbed her attention. Trish quietly said, "You were right when you said the sunset would be gorgeous tonight." The sky had light pink and purple ribbons, with a thicker band of orange closer to the water. It took her breath away.

The two walked in silence for several minutes. It was a comfortable silence, and Trish realized she enjoyed being in Derrick's company.

Breaking the silence, Derrick asked if she wanted to sit on the bench and watch the last few minutes of the sun's descent below the horizon.

Trish had several questions she'd been waiting to ask Derrick, and now was the right time. "Why did you decide to return to Lakeview? I wasn't aware you hadn't been back to our little slice of heaven in years."

"When the Chief of Police position opened, and the house I grew up in went on the market, it seemed the moons were aligning and trying to tell me it was the next step for me to take."

"I'm not sure if you know, my parents have been gone for years, and another family bought the house I grew up in over on Cedar Avenue. When a local real estate agent heard I might be taking the job with the police force, he called me and wondered if I might be interested in the house. At first, I thought he was crazy, but the more I thought about it, the more I was curious to see it. So, on one of my earlier trips back to Lakeview to finalize the deal with the Lakeview Police Department, I toured the house. I was pleasantly surprised it had been extensively renovated over the years and was in excellent condition. The price was right, and I needed a place to live, so I bought it."

Without thinking, Trish gently laid her hand on Derrick's arm. "I heard about the terrible accident your parents were in and their passing. I'm sorry for your loss. I decided not to attend their funerals as I was worried it might have been awkward, and you already had more than enough to handle."

Trish paused for a minute, then continued. "I think it's great you bought your childhood home. I've driven by there a few times, and I love the porch they built across the front and the landscaping. The flower beds are always well-kept, and the array of colors is breathtaking. Do you have a green thumb?"

Derrick chuckled and said, "Absolutely not, but I guess I'll have to learn, especially since you said you liked how the flowerbeds look. The pressure is on."

The sun had finally slipped below the horizon, but the conversation continued with updates about friends they remembered from high school and other local events.

The darkness of the night was offset by the lights along the walkway and the bright moon, but it also created an intimate feeling. During their conversation, her hand slid down Derrick's arm and now rested on his hand.

Trish didn't want to move her hand or break the spell she was feeling, but it was getting late. "I guess it's time to head back to the inn."

Derrick stood up first and reached for her arm to help her stand. Suddenly, they were very close to each other. Trish could feel him looking at her, and their eyes met. His gaze was steady, like he was looking into her soul, but she couldn't seem to move away. She was anchored to the spot, and the tingle started again. Warning bells were going off in her head, so she moved away. But before she could step backward, he pulled her closer and lightly brushed his lips across hers. The kiss was as light as a feather and only lasted a few seconds. Derrick pulled back, but only slightly, and looked down into her big blue eyes again as if asking for permission to kiss her again.

Trish seemed to be in a daze and didn't want the moment to end, and without really thinking about what she was doing, she took a step closer to Derrick, wrapped her arms around his neck, and initiated a deep kiss that went on and on.

When the kiss ended, they stayed locked in each other's arms. Derrick whispered into her ear, "That was unexpected but wonderful. I've wanted to kiss you since I first saw you after returning to Lakeview. The kiss was worth the wait."

Trish's legs were like butter, and she was afraid to let go of Derrick, fearing she might collapse on the walkway, but she steadied herself and stepped back. "I don't know what came over me. I don't typically make out with men on the sidewalk, especially in sight of the inn's windows. It was nice."

"Nice?" Derrick questioned.

"Okay, it was more than nice. It was wonderful. I forgot what a great kisser you were. Maybe that was a fluke. Can we try it one more time?"

"Of course, the local police are here to protect and serve their residents. I'm more than happy to serve this resident."

Although he was having fun with the dialogue, his mood changed as he embraced Trish, and the kiss became more passionate than the last one. It promised more to come and a potential change in their relationship.

After a few more minutes of enjoying another round of kissing, the couple took one last look at the gorgeous moon as it painted varying shades of orange across the lake's surface. As they reached the inn's front door, Derrick was the first to break the spell. "It's been a wonderful evening. Can I call you to set up a date for dinner later this week?"

Now that Trish was less hesitant about pursuing a deeper relationship with Derrick, she raised her chin and looked intently into those gorgeous dark brown eyes. "Absolutely."

Trish walked into the inn with a smile on her face and a song in her heart. As she headed for her room, she took a slight detour and walked over to the large windows in the dining room. With the dark outside, she saw her reflection in the window and realized her hair was a mess, and her lipstick smudged. She raised her hand to her lips and touched them. She wanted to remember how Derrick's lips felt on hers. Her lips were soft, and she wished she was still standing in his embrace. Suddenly, there was a slight chill on her arms, and she realized being in Derrick's arms made her feel warm, cozy, and safe, and she wanted to return to that cocoon as soon as possible.

Not wanting to run into Cassidy or Amanda, she turned around and quickly walked to her suite. She needed a long, hot bath and quiet time to sort through her feelings. She hadn't felt like this in years, and it was all happening so fast. Maybe she should slow down? On the other hand, perhaps the timing was perfect.

CHAPTER EIGHTEEN

Sarah arrived at the shop early the following Monday morning to meet Tom. Trish had called Sarah late Sunday to tell her Tom was coming to the shop. He was determined to find the problem with the erratic electrical issues resulting in the false alarms on the security system.

The system issues were driving everyone crazy, and now Trish was getting heavily fined for the number of false alarms. Trish told Sarah she was so frustrated she even considered removing the security system until the issues were resolved. But her insurance company wouldn't cover her if anything happened.

Sarah heard a knock on the back door, and assuming it was Tom, she hurried to let him in.

Tom was trying to juggle his toolbox, a paper bag, and two cups of coffee, so Sarah reached out the door to take the cups from him.

"I know how much you like those fancy concoctions from The Perk, and Amy was kind enough to make one for you. I don't even know what you call that thing, but I must admit, it sure does smell good. I'm not sure what Amy put in the bag, but again, she said it was your favorite Danish."

Sarah and Tom walked down the hall and into the breakroom, where they put down the items they were carrying. She took the contents from the bag and placed them on a small plate. "Oh boy, Bear Claws." The sweet yeast-raised pastry covered in a thin layer of glazed icing perfectly complimented her Dalgona. "Thank you. These are my favorites." She slid one plate toward Tom along with the regular cup of coffee and took the lid off her Dalgona. She immediately smelled the rich, dark coffee with a hint of chocolate and caramel.

After taking a few bites of the Danish and drinking several gulps of her drink, Sarah tried to decide how to apologize to Tom for jumping to conclusions about his sister, Leah, being his wife.

Before she could speak, Tom quickly blurted out, "Have I done something to offend you? You seem standoffish. I thought we were both feeling a connection, but you backed away. What did I do? I want to know so I can either correct it or we can decide our relationship should stay strictly professional."

Color flooded Sarah's cheeks, "I'm embarrassed, Tom. To sum it up, yes. I was starting to really like you, and the connection between us was growing, but then I overheard the town gossip, Mrs. Lester, introducing Leah to a group of women at The Perk. I misunderstood and thought she said Leah was your wife, and when I saw she was pregnant, I was appalled that you'd be flirting with me when your wife was weeks, if not days, away from giving birth. I jumped to conclusions. Worst of all, I didn't ask or allow you to explain. Please forgive me. I was so wrong."

Tom didn't say anything for so long Sarah was worried he was mad and would walk out of the shop, but instead, he started to laugh. "Oh my. No wonder you backed off. I hope you know you can talk to me about anything. Let's agree we'll always talk to one another if we have questions or concerns. As you can see, making assumptions can potentially lead to missing out. I can't wait to tell Leah this story. I don't think she'll believe me."

Tom took two steps toward Sarah and stopped. "Of course, I'll forgive you."

He reached out, took Sarah's coffee cup out of her right hand, and removed the plate from her left hand. He placed both items on the nearby table. Then, he slowly took two steps closer to her.

Sarah could see his smile had turned into a smoldering look, and leaning in, he lightly pressed his lips on hers. But quickly, the pressure deepened, his arms tightened around her, and Sarah felt a tingling sensation running up and down her whole body. She also thought she heard bells ringing. The couple stayed locked together until Tom moved back slightly, his arms still wrapped around her.

"Wow. I've wanted to do that for several weeks. That kiss was really something, and as much as I hate to admit it, I thought I heard bells ringing."

"I thought I also heard bells ringing," Sarah replied.

Suddenly, they both heard bells ringing again and realized the doorbell on the back door was repeatedly being pushed. Tom remembered he had left his helper outside gathering their tools. Tom hurried to the back door and let his helper inside.

When Tom and his assistant returned to the breakroom, Sarah and Tom looked at each other and suddenly burst out laughing. The helper looked at them like they were crazy. Tom said, "It's an inside joke, but we need to get to work right now. Sarah, I'll find you once we assess the situation and determine what needs to be done next."

Sarah stocked shelves and organized supplies at the checkout counter for the next hour. The work was a bit mindless, and it gave her time to replay the kiss over and over in her mind. She wondered if Tom wanted to repeat the kiss as much as she did. He was a great kisser, and the tingling feeling stayed with her. She knew she was in deep when she daydreamed about more than a few hot kisses.

Sarah was so lost in thought she didn't hear Tom walk up behind her until he called her name, which made her jump.

"I didn't mean to scare you. I wanted to update you on what we found, or in this case, what we didn't find. There weren't any loose connections. Everything looks fine from an electrical perspective."

Tom paused for a moment and then continued, "The next step is to contact the local electric company and have them test your line from the pole at the end of the alley to where it comes into your building. It could be some type of electrical power short at that point. I know this is frustrating, but by going through a process of elimination, we'll find the culprit. Let me know if I can help you with the electric company conversation."

It looked like Tom wanted to say something else, but he hesitated. For once, Sarah remained quiet, giving him time to express his thoughts.

Finally, he started speaking again. "Would you have dinner with me tonight? I've heard great reviews about the food and service at the new Italian restaurant outside town and wanted to try it. I also hear they have the best Tiramisu you've ever tasted."

Sarah replied without hesitation, "Yes, I'd like that, and Italian food is one of my favorite meals."

"How about seven? I could pick you up at home if you'd like," Tom asked.

"Seven works, but please pick me up here at the shop. I'll see you tonight."

After Tom left the shop, Sarah called the local electric company, and they agreed to have someone stop by later in the afternoon. Once the day got rolling, sales were brisk, and even with two other clerks working, they were so busy they barely had time to stop for lunch.

Around two o'clock, the technician from the electric company hoisted his ladder up the side of the building and climbed up the electric pole. Sarah stood in the alley, trying to watch what he was doing, but it wasn't easy to see from her location. She watched the technician retrieve some gadgets from his truck and climb back up the pole. She was hopeful the issue was on the side of the electric company and could be fixed quickly.

Twenty minutes later, the technician approached Sarah and said everything was fine. All the readings were as expected, and the flow of electricity from the city's power pole to the gift shop was smooth. If the shop had trouble with a faulty alarm system, she should contact her alarm company or another electrician to check her inside wiring. He also added many of the old buildings in town had antiquated electrical systems and needed updating.

Sarah paused before responding. She thought the technician was being condescending. If he only knew everything they'd been through, he would understand the look on her face. Trying not to be flippant with the technician, she told him Trish had gone through the expense and frustration of fully updating the electrical system and had a new alarm system installed.

The technician made a few notes on a form attached to his metal clipboard, ripped off the page, and handed it to Sarah. With a wave of his hand, he jumped into his truck and drove off.

Sarah called Trish to give her an update—basically that there was nothing new— and hurried back inside to help with the busier-than-usual number of shoppers. On the one hand, business was booming and no one had mentioned getting a parking ticket for several days. On the other hand, they still didn't know what was causing the false alarms.

Tom arrived at the shop exactly at seven. Sarah had already freshened up her makeup and hair, turned off the lights in the shop, and locked the doors. As she turned on the alarm, she said a small prayer everything would remain quiet and not interrupt her dinner with Tom.

Sarah was surprised to see Tom in a late-model sedan. She had only ever seen him in his Lakeview Electrical Services van. She was also pleasantly surprised to see him walk around to the passenger door and hold it open for her.

Sarah slipped into her seat, and once Tom got in the car and closed his door, she quickly glanced at him. He wore navy blue dockers, a chocolate-brown button-down shirt, and casual loafers. His brown hair was freshly washed, and the color of his shirt made his dark brown eyes shine. He smelled fantastic, something a bit woodsy, and it suited him perfectly.

As they drove down Main Street, Sarah decided the quiet was becoming uncomfortable, so she said, "I've only seen you in your work van. Do you drive your car often?"

Tom smiled. "I learned my lesson about picking dates up in my work van. Not many women want to be seen in a work van, especially when the tagline under our logo says, We Light You Up."

Sarah laughed. She had never noticed the tagline on the side of the van. Now that she knew what it said, she agreed having another vehicle for dates was a good idea.

Less than fifteen minutes later, they were seated at the restaurant. Attillio's had opened earlier in the year and the reviews had been excellent. They featured authentic Italian cuisine, and all the pasta was made from scratch. Sarah appreciated they locally sourced many of their ingredients.

Since Tom had made a reservation, they were seated immediately, even though several other couples were waiting.

Looking around, Sarah noticed the new restaurant was packed. She took a deep breath and the wonderful smells instantly hit her nose and ran to her tastebuds. If the wonderful aroma indicated the taste of the food, they were in for a treat.

"I love Italian food, and it smells delicious in here." Sarah fingered her cloth napkin, admiring the ambiance of the elegant dining room. "Thank you for suggesting the new restaurant. If you hadn't brought me here, it would have been months before my friends and I could try it. Heading up the Artisans Community is rewarding, but as you can imagine, the coordination of events and the diversity of the art often makes it challenging. Plus, my work at Crystal Lake Gifts, which I love, makes for a hectic calendar. My friends are also busy these days, and our get-togethers are getting further apart. As much as we try not to let that happen, it seems life gets in the way."

"I know what you mean." Tom leaned forward. "Moving here, taking over Lakeview Electrical Services, finding a place to live, and helping my sister have taken a toll on my personal life. Don't get me wrong. I enjoy living in Lakeview, and I love the sense of community. The people are so nice, and business is better than I expected. I'm glad I decided to take the leap and move here."

After hesitating for a split second, he added, "I wouldn't have met you if I hadn't moved here. I'm glad I decided to make Lakeview my home."

Before Tom could say anything else, the waiter stopped at their table to take their order.

Sarah was surprised Tom was so open about his feelings. It was all new for her. In retrospect, maybe she overreacted to the kiss at the shop. Perhaps she imagined the tingling in her arms. Did Tom feel it too?

Two hours later, Tom was stuffed. "That meal was delicious. The tableside Caesar salad was impressive, and the homemade spaghetti noodles and sauce…wow, I can't eat another bite. What about you, Sarah?"

"Same here. I had planned to order one of those delicious looking desserts on their dessert cart, but I couldn't even squeeze in a crumb. We'll have to do this again and come for coffee and dessert."

Tom looked at Sarah and said, "I'm hoping you'll go on another date with me. What do you say? How about this weekend?"

"Yes, I'd like that Tom. It's been a delightful evening. Thank you for asking me."

All too soon, the bill was paid, and they were returning to the shop.

When Tom pulled into a parking spot next to Sarah's car, he turned toward her. "Sarah, I have a confession to make. The first time I saw you at the Lakeview Farmers Market, I knew I had to get to know the lady behind those gorgeous emerald-green eyes. I saw you at Crystal Lake Gifts, but you weren't too happy with me when I showed up to get the electricity back on for the grand opening. I saw the fire in your eyes, and it caught my interest. The kisses earlier today sealed the deal. I'm beginning to think you've put a spell on me."

Tom walked around the car, opened the passenger door, and helped guide Sarah out of the car. When she stood up, he closed the few inches of space between them and kissed her again. This time, he lingered, stepped back, took a deep breath, and touched his lips lightly to hers again.

Sarah was lost. The tingling had returned and expanded, running up and down her arms and back. The kisses were passionate yet soft. Her brain seemed to be in a fog. Everything around them disappeared as if it were the two of them alone with no one else around. The kisses continued, and Tom wrapped his arms around her back and pulled her closer. There was heat and the promise of more to come.

Hearing a car horn beep, Sarah returned to the present and realized they were standing on the sidewalk on Main Street kissing like two teenagers. She stepped back, and the cool night air rushed between them, replacing the heat of a few seconds earlier. If it hadn't felt so good, she might have been embarrassed, but she wasn't.

"That was the best dessert I ever had," Sarah said.

Tom looked confused, "But we didn't have dessert."

"Oh yes, we did, and those kisses were the most delicious thing I've ever tasted. I can't wait to have more, but sadly, I've got to get going. I have an early meeting tomorrow, and it's nearly midnight," Sarah said breathlessly.

With one more quick touch of their lips, Tom walked Sarah to her car and waited for her to put it in gear and drive down the street. It was a good thing Tom waited for Sarah to take off, or she might have sat there for another hour replaying the kissing scene repeatedly in her head.

On her way out of town, the last stop light turned red as she approached it. It gave her time to take a deep breath and calm down. She had never believed in love at first sight, but now with Tom, she felt she might be coming around to the idea.

As the light turned green, it reminded Sarah of Tom's comment about her emerald-green eyes, often described as 'green as the fields of Ireland.' Tonight, she was so happy her ancestors passed down her gorgeous green eyes. She recalled her grandmother telling her the largest concentration of people with green eyes was in Ireland. Based on her family's eye color, her grandmother's assessment was correct. She had always loved men with green eyes, but then she remembered that Tom had brown eyes. *But brown eyes are fine when the rest of the package is gorgeous.*

CHAPTER NINETEEN

The following Monday morning, Jack and Cassidy walked into Crystal Lake Gifts a few minutes after they opened. Jack wanted to follow through on his promise to Trish to review the situation with the false alarms and see if he had any suggestions on what might be causing the issues. Cassidy joined him as she wanted to get a gift for her mother, Kate, whose birthday was coming up soon. "Cassidy, you look wonderful, and your pregnancy glow is showing," Trish said as she walked over to Cassidy and hugged her.

"I'm feeling fine, but Jack, my mother hen, is watching me closely. He insisted on driving me here today."

Jack's chest puffed out like a proud papa, and he reached over and gently kissed Cassidy's lips. "Okay, enough of this gushy stuff. Trish and I have work to do."

Cassidy walked over to Sarah. "Can you help me? I'm looking for a unique birthday gift for my mother. She already has everything, so finding something special is getting harder and harder. I was hoping you could suggest something from your artisans' line."

Sarah helped Cassidy look for a gift for Kate while Jack and Trish headed to the back of the store, where the electrical panel and security videotapes were located.

Trish walked Jack through the areas where most of the alarms had triggered, showed him the electrical panel, and left him in the small storage area to review the videotapes. Since the store was open and a few customers were browsing around, Trish excused herself to help customers but promised to return in a few minutes.

When Trish returned, she told Jack, "Sarah had a delivery for Crystal Lake Inn and offered to take Cassidy home since it looked like the research would take a while. Cassidy said she found the perfect gift for her mother and planned to go home and put her feet up. She also said you could stop worrying about her. She's feeling fine."

Trish resumed her spot in the chair next to Jack's, and they refocused on the screen.

An hour later, Jack and Trish's eyes were blurry from watching the videotape recordings, so they decided to stop and get a cup of coffee. As Trish reached over to turn the machine off, Jack said, "Stop." He asked her to rewind the tape backward a few frames.

"Stop right there. Did you see that movement?"

"I didn't see anything," Trish responded.

Jack asked her to rewind the tape again and stop at the point where the timer on the screen showed five-forty-six p.m. last Saturday, which was around the same time as the last false alarm.

"Stop! Look closely at the view of the storage room and then at the left corner of the tarp. What is that tarp covering?" Jack looked at Trish, his investigative mind whirring.

"The tarp is covering some unused furniture and equipment. We never go into that corner of the storage room because there's nothing we use for the shop. Why do you ask? Did you see something?"

Jack took control of the equipment and slowly advanced the video forward about thirty seconds. "Did you see that small furry animal emerge from under the tarp?"

"Oh my gosh, yes, I see it, but I don't know what it is. Do you?"

Jack stopped the recording again so they could get a good look at the small furry animal. They expanded the size of the frozen screen to see the animal better. It was small with reddish-brown fur, a white belly, and chestnut brown stripes down its back.

Jack started laughing, but Trish wasn't amused, "What is that darn thing?"

"It's a chipmunk. Eastern chipmunks are known to live in Maine, so I'm not surprised it's a chipmunk, but I am surprised to see one living in your storage room and not outside. They typically like to live near trees that produce acorns."

"Let's watch a bit more of the video and see what our little furry friend does next," Jack said as he slowly turned the videotape back on.

At first, they lost sight of the chipmunk, but then they saw him scurry from the storage room into the breakroom. He climbed onto the counter and skillfully opened a pack of cheese crackers. It took him several minutes to eat the crackers, but he finished the entire package, and then he nibbled at the crumbs. When he was done, he scampered back to the storage room and ran under the tarp. They watched the film for several more minutes and didn't see the furry animal again. They decided to take a break and headed to the breakroom.

After getting a cup of coffee, he sat at the table. "Have you seen any furry animals around the shop?"

"No, we haven't. Even though I've lived in Maine most of my life, I don't recall seeing a live chipmunk. They are cute little creatures."

"Cute? I don't think I'd call them cute. It's hard to get them out once they get inside your house or building. You'll likely have to call the local animal control office to see if they can help you. Some animals are protected, so you'll have to be careful how you handle their relocation."

"Relocation program? Are you kidding me? I'm not the FBI or the CIA. I don't want to get into a full-blown relocation program. I want the little furry thing gone from my store."

"Trish, I hate to tell you this, but if you have one chipmunk, you probably have a dozen or more. Even though chipmunks tend to be solitary animals, during mating season, they like to live in a group or what is called a scurry. Be careful and leave them to the professionals. During mating season, chipmunks tend to be territorial and won't care that you're their landlord."

Trish threw her hands up and said, "Are you kidding me? I have the perfect trifecta— parking meters, false alarms, and now let's add mating chipmunks to the list." They both chuckled at her comment.

Jack picked up his coffee cup, "Let's finish our coffee and watch more of the videotape to see where our furry friend is going other than the breakroom. When you speak to the animal control office, any information you can provide to them will be useful. I'll take a couple of screenshots, which might be helpful."

Once they finished their coffee, they returned to the storage room and rewound the tape. Jack had a hunch but wanted to do more research before he discussed it with Trish. She was upset, and he didn't want to add to her aggravation unless he had proof.

Trish was called to the front of the store to help a customer with a large order from her new designer clothes section, so she left Jack to do his research.

A few minutes later, Trish returned to the breakroom to find Jack leaning back in the office chair with a big smile. It was clear he'd discovered something interesting on the tapes.

"You'll never guess what I found. Go ahead and try to guess." Jack teased.

"How do I know what you found? Please tell me. What did you find on the older tapes?"

Jack hesitated for a second longer, then spoke, sharing his discovery. "I looked back a few weeks and decided to look at the dates and times of your false alarms. I saw our furry friends running from the storage room to the area around the electrical panel at the exact time the alarm went off. After watching the tapes a bit longer, here's what I found."

Jack pointed to the screen, and Trish leaned over to get a better look.

"I don't believe it." Trish looked shocked. "They're storing acorns in a hollow place in the wall behind the electrical panel. That explains why the electrician found some old acorn shells behind the box when he did the rewiring. They must be storing their acorns there in preparation for winter. What do we do now?"

"Let's look at the wall in the storage room that backs up to the wall behind the electrical box. Maybe we can see their hiding place."

Sure enough, as soon as they moved the tarp a bit and inched slowly between the old furniture and the wall in the old portion of the store, they saw the gap in the drywall. The insulation was missing. The hole was about the size of a one-pound coffee can. Looking into the opening, they saw it was full of acorns. They didn't hear anything scurrying about, which, for the moment, made Trish happy. She knew they were hiding somewhere in the area and wasn't looking forward to having them run across her path when she was in the store alone.

Next, they walked down the hallway by the back door where the electrical panel was located, opened the panel, slightly pushed on the frame, and out popped a couple of acorns.

"As far as I can piece the situation together, the chipmunks are collecting acorns, bringing them into your shop, and storing them in the gap they created in the wall," Jack said. "The acorns in the electrical panel caused enough interference to trigger the alarm. The electrical shortages stopped once Tom put extra installation behind the panel, but the alarm interference continued.

"Once you get rid of the chipmunks, you get rid of your alarm problem. Although it might not be as easy as it sounds."

Trish looked dismayed. "At least now we know what's causing the issues. And thinking about it further, I bet our little furry friends were used to running all over the shop while we were under renovations. If enough of them were in here, they could have knocked over the lamp, which broke the glass display case. Since they're apparently so fast and like to hop from one thing to another, that could also account for the clothes on the hangers getting lopsided. We already saw one of them eating an entire pack of cheese crackers, which accounts for the crumbs in the kitchen.

"I'm not sure I can get the insurance company to agree with me, but if you can email me a couple of those video clips, I'll send them to the company, along with our hypothesis, and see what they think."

Trish reached over and gave Jack a big hug. "I was right about your experience in writing intriguing spy novels. Your ability to follow the trail, or in this case, the acorns, helped us get to the bottom of the problem. Thanks so much."

"While I waited for you to return from helping your customer, it dawned on me that the downtown renovation project a few years ago added all those beautiful Red Oak trees along Main Street. The Red Oak is the most common tree in Maine, so it made sense that was the type of tree they planted. These trees have an abundance of acorns, hence the chipmunks.

"Luckily, none of the chipmunks were electrocuted, but if they start chewing on your wiring again or making a nest in the wall, it could cause a fire hazard. It would be best if you sorted this out quickly. Also, it would be good to contact your friend at the local police department and report the unusual criminals."

Trish shook her head up and down with an exasperated look on her face, "Absolutely. I'll start making calls now. These phone calls should be interesting. I hope no one thinks I'm a bit bonkers. Thanks again for all your help."

Jack left the store. As he walked to his car, parked a couple of spots down from the shop, he noticed acorns on the ground near one of the gorgeous Red Oak trees. It made him smile. He was glad he could help Trish solve her mystery. He hoped her insurance company would reconsider their position and reimburse her for the damages.

As Jack started to open his car door, he noticed a piece of paper on his windshield. He grabbed the paper. It was a parking ticket. Looking closer, he saw he was fined for 'time-expired' on the meter, although he had used the parking app and paid for four hours. Looking at his watch, he confirmed he had only been in the shop for three hours.

Interestingly, I helped solve one mystery, and now I'm a member of the 'Time Expired' Club of Lakeview, which is not a club I want to be a member of. Jack intended to stop by the local Police Station on his way out of town and add his complaint to the pile he'd heard they already had. Wait till Cassidy heard how his day went.

Since Trish had called Derrick earlier and explained what she and Jack discovered about the chipmunk bandits, Derrick offered to stop by the shop around closing time and give her the insurance paperwork, which he'd updated with the new official police report and conclusion. He was reasonably sure the insurance company would call him once they read the updated report. It was a good thing Jack emailed him several video clips. It would make the conversation with the insurance company go a lot smoother.

Trish was so relieved the mystery was solved. There was still the problem of getting the chipmunks out of the store, but she had already placed a call to a firm that specialized in relocating these types of animals. She was so excited that when she saw Derrick walk into the shop, she immediately ran over to him and planted a sweet kiss on his cheek.

Derrick looked around the shop and didn't see anyone, and in response, he pulled Trish into an embrace and initiated a long and passionate kiss that left her breathless.

Trish could feel the flush rising from her neck to her cheeks, so she started to step back to cool off, but before she could loosen Derrick's embrace, she heard someone clearing their throat, quickly forcing them apart.

"Oh my. We shouldn't be standing in front of the window kissing," Trish said, a little breathless.

Turning around to see who cleared their throat, Trish saw that Sarah and Tom had walked into the room. Tom quickly stepped in front of Sarah and gave her a quick kiss on the lips. Sarah is now the one blushing. Tom stepped back and said, "I always try to follow the guidance of the local police department and follow their example. I guess kissing is the order of the day."

Sarah tried to hide her embarrassment, "I came in through the back door to close out the register for the day, and Tom stopped by. I didn't realize Derrick was also visiting."

Trish was still stunned so Derrick spoke up. "Why don't the two of you join Trish and me at the Lakeview Diner for dinner, and we'll fill you in on the Chipmunk Bandit. If I hadn't seen the evidence Jack and Trish shared with me with my own eyes, I'm not sure I would have believed them. Let's go eat. All this kissing has given me a big appetite."

CHAPTER TWENTY

The sky was morphing from the dark indigo of the wee hours of the morning through various hues of blue. As Derrick left the Lakeview Police Station, the sky was a gorgeous shade similar to the color known as Robin's Egg Blue on the color swatches at the local paint store.

Derrick loved this time of day. It was the best time to start his patrol. The streets of Lakeview were beginning to wake up. A few people were enjoying their morning walks or runs. Delivery trucks rolled into town. He saw the produce truck stop at the Lakeview Diner, while the fresh flower delivery van stopped in front of Crystal Lake Flowers. A little further down the street, he saw a driver putting large boxes on a conveyor belt, which then pushed them through the big roll-up door at Lakeview Hardware. Everything was as it should be, which always made a police officer happy.

Derrick drove around the four streets that made up Lakeview's downtown area, and at six-thirty he stopped at The Perk to grab a fresh cup of coffee and one of their delicious Bear Claws. He was surprised at the number of people already waiting in line, but Amy and her crew quickly worked through the crowd. He took his food outside and sat on one of the benches that lined Main Street.

He was listening to his police radio when the squeaky wheel of a large water container on a cart caught his attention. The workers had long, telescoping watering wands with bent ends. He was curious about what the wands were used for. He saw the worker reach up to water the hanging baskets attached to the streetlights along the street. *That's a clever idea.* The long wands made it easy to reach and thoroughly water the baskets.

The process was time-consuming, which reminded Derrick of the last town budget meeting and the debate around how much the town spent each year for its annual 'beautification' project. While the investment was steep, the flowers were gorgeous, and the streets and sidewalks were well-maintained.

The efforts seemed to be paying off. He'd heard compliments from many residents and tourists. They loved the town's cleanliness, brightly lit streets, inviting storefronts, and the gorgeous flowers spilling over the edges of the hanging baskets. Derrick realized he felt a renewed sense of pride in his hometown.

After watering the dozen hanging baskets along Main Street, the maintenance workers jumped back in their truck and headed toward the maintenance yard behind the Town Hall building.

Derrick finished his coffee break and walked to his car, parked halfway up the block from The Perk. As he stepped under one of the hanging baskets, he was startled to feel water droplets hit the back of his neck and run down his uniform shirt. He quickly moved away from the basket, grabbed the napkins around his coffee cup, and wiped his collar to get any excess water.

As he looked at the next basket, located right before the spot where his police car was parked, he saw a small stream of excess water running out of the saucer on the bottom of the flowerpot and down the light pole to puddle on the cement at its base.

He made a mental note to walk around that basket and not under it to avoid getting drenched.

Cassidy was ready for a busy day at the inn. Several families were checking out after a long weekend during which the weather had been gorgeous, especially for late Spring in Maine.

Meanwhile, a small group of business travelers were checking in. Cassidy discovered this group of former co-workers had worked together for years and had gone their separate ways in business yet remained close personal friends. They got together annually for a few days, and during football season, they frequently tailgate at their hometown team, the Philadelphia Eagles.

The group was friendly and asked for assistance booking spa appointments for all six. "I'm happy to book your appointments at the Lakeview Spa. It's a mile from here and has a wonderful view of the lake but from a different vantage point than our inn. Since it's already three o'clock today, would it be better to book for tomorrow morning?"

The person who seemed to be the spokesperson for the group said tomorrow would be perfect, so Cassidy excused herself to call the spa and make the appointments since they tended to go fast.

Cassidy returned to the front desk, "I was able to book appointments for ten tomorrow morning. The spa has expanded and was fully renovated last winter and now has a dozen treatment rooms, each with a fireplace and an overall feeling of calm and relaxation. I know you'll enjoy your experience. Would you also like me to book a dinner reservation for you for tonight?"

The five women and one man looked at each other, and the spokesperson said, "We've heard great reviews about the food here at the inn, so we'd like to eat here tonight if you can accommodate us. Let's say seven. Please make the reservation for seven people, not six."

"That works. I've booked one of the larger tables by the windows, so you'll have a fantastic view of the lake and the sunset. Is there anything else I can do before you head to your rooms? If you need anything, don't hesitate to let me know."

The group headed toward the elevator, and Cassidy could hear them laughing about something that happened at the airport earlier in the afternoon. She thought it was interesting how they didn't even speak among themselves about dinner but had some shared understanding, and it was silently agreed they were having dinner at the inn. As she thought about it, she realized that she, Amanda, and Trish had been friends for so long they often didn't need words to convey what they wanted to say or do. It brought a smile to Cassidy's face. She truly hoped this group enjoyed their stay at the inn.

Finally, the check-ins were completed, and the lobby was quiet. Cassidy decided to pop into the kitchen to see if Amanda or Peter needed help. Something delicious delighted her nose when she pushed through the door.

"What is that delicious aroma?"

Amanda wiped her hands on a towel beside the sink and turned around. "That's tonight's special—Crown Roast of Pork with stuffed diced apples, herbs, breadcrumbs, brown sugar, and dried cranberries. And, of course, Peter is dressing it up with those little chef hats for the tops of the roast spears. He is also making several side dishes, including lobster macaroni and cheese, homemade yeast dinner rolls, and chocolate croissants for dessert."

"Yummy. By the way, I booked seven more for dinner tonight. That makes a full house. Will you need extra serving help? I can always stick around and help with dinner service," Cassidy offered.

"Absolutely not," Amanda replied quickly. "You're under orders to take it easy, and being on your feet for another three hours tonight isn't taking it easy. We'll be fine. Go ahead and wrap up your day. We'll see you in the morning."

Cassidy started to walk out of the kitchen but turned around. "We are fully booked next week, and I think we need to go over staffing and menus."

Before Cassidy could even make it halfway across the room, Amanda met her, gently turned her around, escorted her to the front desk, grabbed Cassidy's purse, and ushered her out the front door. "I'll see you in the morning," Amanda said with a fake stern face. "Do I need to call Jack to come and get you?"

"No. No. No. I'm going. Thanks for being a good friend." With those parting words, Cassidy got into her car and drove the short distance to her cabin by the lake.

"Phew! Dinner was delicious, but a full dining room made for a hectic evening," Peter said, turning toward Amanda, who was busy wiping down counters and collecting linens for the laundry. I'm glad we're down to a handful of guests finishing their dessert and coffee. It will allow me to do some prep for breakfast tomorrow."

With her arms full, Amanda headed for the laundry room but was stopped when Peter grabbed her, put his arms around her, and passionately kissed her.

"Hey, you made me drop some of the dirty linens." Amanda stooped down to pick them up and started to walk away again. Peter quickly grabbed her, took the linens away from her, sat them on a table, and pulled Amanda into his arms.

"You have no idea how hard it is to resist kissing you all day. It's a wonder my cooking hasn't suffered from neglect," Peter teased as he held Amanda tight in his arms. Quickly, the playful kiss turned into something more passionate, and Amanda responded, wrapping her arms around Peter's waist. The couple continued to enjoy this stolen time together. When Peter's hands started roaming under Amanda's shirt, they heard her name being called by the one server left in the dining room.

Amanda pulled back a little and looked up at Peter. "I need to go and see who needs me. Let's continue this later when we're in our apartment. I think it will be a long night," she said, kissing Peter's cheek.

Walking into the dining room, she heard loud laughter. Looking across the room, she saw only one table was still occupied. It seemed like the business travelers were having a blast.

Amanda checked with the server to determine what she needed and was told the business travelers had asked to speak to the dining room manager. The server added that when only six guests were seated for dinner and only six placed dinner orders, she started to remove the extra place setting like they typically did. "As I picked up the silverware, all six guests spoke at once and asked me to leave it. I was so startled that I dropped the silverware, and it hit the plate, making an awful sound. I'm sorry. I didn't want you to think I wasn't following our guidelines." The server seemed a bit nervous.

Amanda smiled at the server to let her know it was okay and that she'd talk to the guests, and then she walked across the dining room.

"Hi, I'm Amanda, the manager of the inn. I understand you asked to speak to me. How can I be of service?"

One of the women in the group spoke up. "We wanted to share something with you. It might sound like an unusual request when we ask for a reservation for seven rather than six, but it's customary for our annual trip, and we hope you don't mind."

The woman stopped talking and looked at her friends around the table. At that point, the only male in the group started speaking and explained their request. "You see, there are six of us on this trip, but seven were originally in our group. Our good friend, JD, passed away a few years ago, and we miss him. He had a big personality, so losing him left a gap. For a while, it was too painful to get together without him. It took us a while to find our footing, and we realized JD would want us to continue our close friendship, travel together, and enjoy life. We will always keep JD in our hearts. For fun, we started to make reservations for seven again, although only six of us were there. For some strange reason, this seems to lift our spirits, keep JD in our hearts, and lessen the pain."

The man continued, "We don't want to confuse you or your staff when we make dinner reservations for seven and only six show up. We'd appreciate it if you did place settings for seven."

The group was quiet while Amanda considered their request. Even though it was unusual, she quickly understood how it would help them feel closer to their friend even though he was no longer with them.

"I understand, and I'll alert the staff. We'll try our best to honor your request." Before walking away, she asked, "Is there anything else I can help you with this evening?"

One of the women in the group said, "Yes, there is one more thing. Can you tell us if The Book Nook is close enough to walk to? One of our friends released a new book last week, and we want to see if it's in the bookstore. We want to take our picture holding her latest best seller, *Friends Here and Gone.* We can't wait to see if we are mentioned in the book, but on the other hand, we are slightly anxious about what stories she might have shared. We've lived and traveled in several countries over the years of our friendship, so there's lots of material for her to use."

"Yes, The Book Nook is in the middle of Main Street. It is walkable from the inn. They open at ten in the morning. While there, you might also want to check out books by Jack Burnett. He writes under the pen name of Thomas J. Burnett and is a best-selling author of international spy books. His wife, who happens to be the owner of this inn, is my best friend. Cassidy and Jack are expecting their first child. We are all so excited for them."

Amanda smiled with pride and continued. "While I seem to be doing an advertisement for our town, you should also check out Crystal Lake Gifts at 300 Main Street, next door to The Book Nook. It's a lovely gift shop with a designer clothing line and crafts made by our local artisans' group. We get terrific feedback from our guests. They seem to love shopping there. They will also ship your packages to your homes for you.

If you stop by, tell them Amanda Blake sent you. I'm good friends with the shop owner, Trish Cavanaugh. Lakeview is a small town. While I don't know everyone, I know most shop owners. The Perk is a cute little coffee and bake shop across the street from the gift shop. Walking along Main Street is a pleasant way to discover what our town has to offer."

Amanda started to walk away but quickly stopped when one of the women in the group asked her a final question. "Is there a hot tub or a gazebo by the lake?" The members of the groups were trying not to laugh at the question, which seemed to have a deeper meaning than on the surface.

"No, there isn't. But we do have a covered pavilion and paddle boats. You can also rent kayaks during the day. At six each evening, you should join us on the front porch for our Sit-n-Sip. We serve light refreshments, you can mingle with other guests, and enjoy the gorgeous views of the lake and the setting sun. There are also benches along the walkway around the lake which is well-lit, so feel free to stroll after dinner." With no more questions from the group, Amanda wished them a good stay in Lakeview and walked back to the kitchen. As she walked away, she heard a member of the group say, "I wonder if she thinks we're crazy? I'm sure JD is looking down at us and laughing his head off. He'd love making us look foolish, but he'd also love that we continue to include him in spirit. Let's take a walk down to the lake. I could use some exercise to walk off the fantastic meal before going to bed."

Amanda thought about what had been said, and although it was an odd request, it was sweet. She'd post the note in their daily communications with the staff.

When Amanda walked back into the kitchen, she noticed the lights were off except for the one wall sconce they kept on at night, and everything was clean and organized for the next day. She assumed Peter was energized to hurry with the cleanup so they could continue where they left off.

Amanda went to the apartment, and as soon as she closed the door behind her, she heard the shower running, which gave her an idea. Since she also needed to shower before bed, she decided it would be energy-efficient if she joined Peter in the shower—or at least that was the excuse she told herself.

She walked quietly down the hall, slipped off her grungy clothes, opened the glass door, and slipped into the shower.

Peter was momentarily surprised but didn't say anything. No words were needed. They immediately connected with each other's needs, and nature took over. In the end, the shower lasted longer than usual, and it didn't turn out to be energy efficient, but who was counting water usage at a time like this? It was the blissful end to a hectic day, which made the coupling so much more passionate.

CHAPTER TWENTY-ONE

April turned into May, which quickly turned into June, and before you could snap your fingers, June turned into July. The summer months gave credence to Maine's nickname of Vacationland, which had been proudly displayed on Maine license plates since 1936. The towns, lakes, forests, and camps overflowed with vacationers.

Some families had called Maine their summer home for generations. With an average population of 1.3 million residents, the influx of forty million visitors, most of whom visited between June and September, pushed businesses to the overflow stage. Lakeview was no different.

Trish and Sarah took a coffee break to review the plans for the upcoming Fourth of July holiday, which happened to be on a Saturday this year and meant even larger crowds in downtown Lakeview. They'd ordered extra stock and had additional summer help on hand.

Trish pulled out her laptop and went over the detailed spreadsheet she used to keep all the details organized. "The parade runs along Main Street in the morning, with picnics at midday and fireworks in the evening held in the park. That's the schedule. As usual, we'll be closed on the fourth, but we'll open early on the third and stay open late that night, which takes advantage of the extra crowds in town for the holiday festivities. It's a long day, but one we all look forward to each year. I'm so glad we're closed on the Fourth and can take advantage of all the events."

"By the way, will Tom join the festivities? How's the situation going between the two of you?"

Sarah's entire face lit up at the mention of Tom. "Yes, Tom asked me to join his family for the picnic and fireworks at the park. It will be his sister Leah, his brother-in-law Sam, and, of course, little Ellie. Sam said he would feel better if Tom joined them in case he was called away for a medical emergency. That way, Leah and Ellie wouldn't be left alone, and Tom could drive them home. Leah is getting close to her delivery date."

Sarah continued, "I'm excited to spend more time with Tom's family and get to know them better. Tom offered to take Ellie home with him for the night to give Sam and Leah a night alone before the new baby arrived. He asked me to help him settle Ellie for the night at his house. It will also give us some time to spend together. I'm looking forward to all the festivities on July Fourth."

"How is Leah feeling?" Trish asked.

"Leah shared with me this pregnancy was much easier than her first one with Ellie. She had a short bout of morning sickness early on and nothing out of the ordinary the past few months. She did say she'd be glad when she could see her feet again.

She and Sam have been working on the nursery. It's painted in pastels with animal wallpaper, white curtains, dark wood furniture, and the cutest baby clothes hanging in the closet. The room sounds adorable, although I haven't seen it yet."

Trish looked over at Sarah, surprised to see the dreamy look on her face. "I don't want to be too nosy, but that look on your face tells me you might be thinking about children in your future. Is it getting serious between you and Tom?"

"Yes, we are getting a little more serious than I first expected," Sarah said softly. "We spend a lot of time together, but our schedules often prevent us from being together as much as we'd like. We enjoy many of the same things, like hiking and canoeing. We are planning a winter ski trip to Sugar Loaf."

Sarah got that dreamy look again. "At first, I was trying to take the relationship slower, but our feelings have deepened, and we recently started talking about a future together. We haven't used the "L" word yet, but I think we're getting there quickly, yet a bit afraid to say it out loud. We've both had bad experiences in the romance department and are treading carefully.

Tom brings out the best in me, and he's claimed my heart. My mother always told me I'd know when the right one came along, and it's clear Tom's the one."

"Oh, Sarah, I'm so happy for you," Trish gave her friend a hug. "Getting to know Tom better through the double dates we've shared has been great, and it allowed Tom and Derrick to become friends. I know they enjoy golfing together. That's been a relief because I don't care to shuffle around a hot golf course chasing a little ball all summer. With their new friendship, Derrick has a good golf buddy."

The two women continued to swap boyfriend stories and finally got back to finalizing the holiday schedule. The next few days would be hectic, but the entire town was ready for a fun day of relaxation, food, fireworks, and spending time with family and friends.

Saturday morning, the fourth, was a gorgeous day. The sky was a vivid blue with no clouds in sight. The forecast was for a high of seventy-five degrees and sunny. The evening would be perfect for fireworks, with clear skies and temperatures in the low sixties.

The morning festivities started in the park at ten o'clock, with Lakeview's Mayor giving a brief speech (well, brief in his mind), followed by the Lakeview High School Chorus singing The Star-Spangled Banner.

An antique Tin Lizzy carrying various town dignitaries started the parade. The parade was filled with music from the local high school band, followed by freshly waxed fire trucks and homemade floats carrying members of the local 4H and various clubs. Children were excited to see the clowns on stilts, dogs dressed in comical outfits, and a group of scouts passing out lollipops.

People gravitated to the park during the afternoon to enjoy an old-fashioned picnic. The park was a favorite spot, and blankets and folding chairs crowded the space. The special picnic hampers supplied by the inn could be seen peppered across the park.

The hampers resembled an old-fashioned woven basket, with handles and plenty of room to pack a meal, blanket, and drinks. A customized brass plate added to the front, reminded people to return them to the inn.

Initially, the hampers were from Cassidy's collection of antique hampers, and what started as a convenient way for the inn to provide lunches for their guests to take to the lake soon became a great marketing tool. Eventually, the hampers became so popular that keeping up with the demand was hard. So, Cassidy made a deal with LACE to make reproductions of the original antique baskets and changed the brass label to read, Visit Lakeview, Maine. Trish added them to her inventory at Crystal Lake Gifts, and they continued to be good sellers. Cassidy finally put her personal antique hampers back in the attic for safekeeping. Occasionally, she'd use them as decorations around the inn, filling them with holiday items or Halloween pumpkins and holding blankets near the firepits in the fall.

The park offered multiple areas where children and adults could join in games of volleyball, horseshoes, croquet, and wiffleball. The playground had recently been extended, and crushed rubber was added as a safe place for the kids to land should anyone take a fall.

As the day turned into late afternoon, families cleaned up from their picnics and you could see several sleeping tots wrapped in light blankets. A few people were stretched out reading, and other groups had pulled their folding chairs into haphazard circles so they could enjoy catching up with each other.

It was an iconic day. The entire country celebrated its birthday, and this was evident across America. Looking across the park, you noticed a sea of red, white, and blue and the smiling faces of those attending.

At dusk, the town employees lit small firepits, and people readied for the fireworks. The smell of freshly popped popcorn filled the air. The crowd started to settle down and waited for the skies to darken.

A few minutes later, the first fireworks were launched and lit the sky with a rainbow of colors. One after the other, each launch silhouetted the dark sky and captured the applause of those watching. As always, the fireworks were breathtaking, and everyone in the crowd was oohing and aahing at the gorgeous display of colors, shapes, and sounds. And all too soon, the festivities were over.

"WOW! Another fantastic firework display. It was a great day. I think everyone enjoyed themselves," Trish remarked as she packed up the last of their picnic items.

Looking across the park, Trish observed people were filing out quickly, but a few small groups still lingered behind. "Now it's time to get everyone safely out of the park and on their way home. I'm glad Tom and Sarah took sweet little sleeping Ellie home right before the fireworks finale to avoid the traffic."

Derrick spoke up. "My deputy sent me a radio message saying that Main Street is backed up, even though our deputies are directing traffic. It should take about fifteen minutes to clear it out. That gives me enough time to walk around the park and ensure everyone is gone and all the firepits have been extinguished."

Trish looked at Leah and saw the day had taken its toll on her. She looked tired, her feet were slightly swollen, and she was constantly rubbing her back.

Leah spoke up. "I want to thank you again for offering to let me stay with you to see the fireworks when Sam got called to an emergency at the hospital. He insisted he take me home, but the fireworks hadn't started. As much as I love that my husband is so dedicated to taking care of babies in distress, it often means Ellie and I don't get to enjoy outings like these. It seems babies are born when they decide to be and not when it's convenient for the parents or the doctors."

"We need to get our little momma home. She looks ready to fall asleep," Trish said so Derrick would get started on his rounds and they could head out and get Leah home.

Looking at his watch, Derrick realized it took longer than he intended to close the park and put chains across the entrances. Twenty minutes had passed since he left Trish and Leah. He stepped up his pace and quickly walked toward his car.

He was surprised Trish had opted to sit in the back seat with Leah. He assumed it was so they could easily talk to pass the time. He'd tell Trish to stay in the backseat and tease them he was their chauffeur for the evening. He removed his hat so he could use it to make a salute-type jester and say he was at their service. It would add some fun to the evening and maybe make Leah laugh. She seemed a bit down since her husband had been called away to the hospital.

Derrick walked up to the back door of his police car and opened it. It took him a minute to fully realize what he saw and heard.

CHAPTER TWENTY-TWO

Leah was lying across the backseat, straining and panting. "What's happening?" Derrick asked, shaking his head to ensure he understood the scene.

Derrick looked at Trish. She was pale, and it was clear she was shaking. "I think it should be obvious. We're having a baby who wants to appear sooner than expected. I called 911, and they're on the way."

Trish stopped and took a deep breath before continuing, "We all need to remain calm. Derrick, I assume you've had training in delivering a baby outside of the hospital. This situation wasn't covered in my Girl Scout's manual." It was clear Trish was desperately trying to appear calm. "I'm not sure what we should be doing to help Leah."

"It all happened so fast. I noticed Leah rubbing her back several times over the past hour, and when we got in the car, she said it was worse, so we stepped out of the car so she could walk around. And after a few steps, her water broke. I had the blanket we used at the park, so I slipped it under her and helped her get into the back seat. Two minutes later, her contractions started coming fast and furious."

After an agonizing contraction and showing signs of difficulty maintaining steady breathing, Leah yelled she couldn't hold off pushing much longer. The baby was coming.

"Did you call Dr. Foster?" Derrick yelled over his shoulder as he hit a button on his keychain that opened the trunk. He grabbed the first aid kit containing the basics and several pairs of surgical gloves. He also found an unused blanket still in the plastic bag and several small bottles of hand sanitizer. He used a whole bottle to clean his hands and forearms.

"Leah called Sam but got his voicemail. I then called the hospital, and they said he was performing a difficult infant surgery. They couldn't disturb him but would have someone standing by to alert him as soon as the surgery was over, and they'd have a police cruiser standing by to get him to us.

But it doesn't look like Sam is the one going to deliver this baby unless he arrives in the next few minutes." As soon as Trish finished her sentence, Leah made a gut-wrenching sound and said she had to push.

Seeing Trish start to panic, Derrick leaned over and whispered into her ear, "We are going to deliver this baby. I need your help, so don't flake out on me now. I need you to help Leah by sliding in behind her and gently leaning her forward when she pushes. I'm so glad you're here to help me. You can do this, Trish."

And with that, Derrick jumped into action. He helped Leah slide forward to allow Trish to slide in behind her. He took a minute to speak slowly and calmly to Leah. "I wouldn't say I've delivered as many babies as your husband, but this isn't my first delivery. If we work together, we can get through this." Derrick draped Leah with the blanket from the seat and looked to see how her labor was progressing. To his surprise, the baby's head was already crowning.

In a flurry of actions and calmly coaching Leah through several big pushes, he told her she needed one more big push. Trish helped Leah lean forward to gather extra strength, and she pushed so hard that the baby finally slid smoothly into Derrick's big hands. The few seconds it took to hear the baby cry were the longest in Derrick's life. The baby made good use of his healthy lungs and started crying. Derrick looked up at Leah and saw tears of joy silently sliding down her face. He took a deep breath, and his body relaxed.

Derrick was surprised to feel someone tap him on the shoulder. Turning his head toward the door, he thankfully saw Leah's husband, Dr. Foster, leaning into the car and saying, "Hi, Derrick. I'll take over from here. If you can guide the EMTs to pull over next to your car, that would be great." Derrick quickly moved aside and gently handed the baby to Sam. Derrick backed out of the car.

Sam looked down at his new son, who seemed content to be in his arms. With a look of joy and love, he leaned over and kissed his wife. "Leah, I'm so sorry I wasn't here when you needed me. I almost missed this event, but I'm here now. Let's see if little Elijah and you are okay. I see ten fingers and ten toes and hear healthy lungs." He checked Leah's heart rate and blood pressure, then turned toward Derrick and Trish. "It's a good thing you had these fantastic friends here to help you through this. I don't know how we'll repay you for what you did. Thank you from the bottom of our hearts."

Dr. Foster swaddled baby Elijah into a small blanket he had brought from the hospital and laid him on Leah's chest so she could get a better look at her new son.

Derrick helped Trish get out of the car and walked her to a nearby picnic table. He could see that she was shaking so badly he thought she might pass out. He quickly helped her sit down, removed his jacket, put it around her shoulders, and sat beside her. "Trish, you were wonderful. I'm so glad you were here to help us. Maybe you missed your calling and should have been a nurse or doctor."

"Oh no. I'm fine being a businesswoman. I was scared and so thankful you were here. You were so gentle with Leah. It made what could have been a bad situation into an excellent outcome."

"I need to step away for a minute if you're sure you're okay." Trish said she was fine so Derrick returned to the car to let Dr. Foster know the ambulance had arrived and the EMTs had the stretcher waiting.

Dr. Foster kissed his wife and son again, his emotions spilling over into tears. "Let's get you two to the hospital," he whispered.

As the EMTs carefully helped move Leah and baby Elijah to the stretcher, Dr. Foster turned to Derrick. "In the commotion, I forgot to ask. I assume Tom has Ellie, but I wanted to check before we left for the hospital."

"Yes, they already planned for Ellie to spend the night at her uncle's house. She fell asleep before the fireworks ended, so Sarah and Tom took her home. She was zonked out. You might want to call Tom and let him know what happened. I'm sure Ellie will be thrilled in the morning to hear her baby brother has arrived.

"By the way, I'll escort the ambulance to the hospital. I'll be ready when you are. And it was my pleasure to help Leah and little Elijah. It's not my first delivery, but it was the first one in a squad car. I'm sure I'll remember it for a long time."

The two men shook hands, and Dr. Foster stepped over to the ambulance as the EMTs lifted the stretcher inside.

Derrick went back to Trish at the picnic table. He noticed tears were still running down her cheeks. Since Trish was still wearing his jacket, he leaned down and reached into the pocket. He pulled out a pack of tissues. He stooped down to meet her eyes and dabbed her face with the tissue.

"Hey, what are the tears for Trish? Everything is fine. Baby Elijah has all his fingers and toes, and his lungs seem in perfect working order, as proven by the loud crying. Leah seemed to be fine, and you know they are in excellent hands since Dr. Foster is a Pediatric Specialist at the hospital's Neonatal Unit."

Derrick pulled Trish into a standing position and put his arms around her. She was still shaking. Gently, he pulled her forward and brushed a kiss across her lips. When Trish leaned into him, it was all the encouragement he needed. Emotions were running high. He deepened the kiss, and it quickly turned into something more passionate. It spoke of the fire she sparked in his body, and the kiss lingered.

"I hate to end this, but I'm escorting the ambulance to the hospital. One of my deputies is taking you home. I'll have some extra paperwork to complete tonight, so I'll say goodnight now." He leaned back for another kiss and motioned for his deputy to join them.

"Please escort Ms. Cavanaugh to Crystal Lake Inn. She's a little shaky, so hold her arm until you get her in the car. Consider her special cargo."

So far, Trish hadn't uttered a word, but she took the deputy's arm and started to walk away. Suddenly, she released the deputy's arm, ran back to Derrick, put her arms around him, leaned up, and planted a kiss on his lips. Since it caught him off guard, he slightly stumbled backward.

Finally, Trish found her voice. "You were wonderful tonight. Do you know how sexy it is to see a big, strong man deliver a baby? It's a shame you have to work late tonight. I want to give you a proper thank you. Hey, I just remembered that tomorrow is Sunday. I'd love for you to join us at the inn for brunch?" She stepped back a few steps, gave Derrick a big wink, and walked back over to the young deputy, who was trying desperately to hide the smile on his face.

As Trish and the deputy started to walk away, Derrick called out, "Deputy, if you want to protect your job, you'll get Ms. Cavanagh home safely post haste. Is that understood?"

Without hesitation, the deputy wiped the smile from his face and replied, "Yes, sir."

Derrick hurried to his car, turned on the flashing red lights, and escorted the ambulance out of the park. As he drove, his thoughts were all over the place. The adrenaline rush, which helped him through the delivery, was running out, but it didn't diminish his pride in his job and the excellent training he'd received. He was honored to be able to help deliver the baby. If the truth was known, he'd also been scared. What if something had gone wrong? He knew better than to second guess himself when an emergency was over. It helped to recall the comment Trish made. She called him strong and sexy. Hopefully, he was finally getting somewhere with her. The thought sent a new surge of adrenaline through him. *That should keep me going.*

CHAPTER TWENTY-THREE

Derrick decided to take the early shift on Sunday morning so one of his deputies could join his family at a church event. As usual, when he took the early shift, he started before the sun rose over the lake, and after finishing up some paperwork, he headed to The Perk for a light breakfast—something to hold him over until he joined Trish and the others at the inn.

"Good morning, Chief Williams. What can I get for our town hero this morning," Amy called as Derrick walked into The Perk. "We heard about your special delivery last night. Everyone is so grateful that you were there to help deliver little Elijah. Have whatever you want this morning. It's on the house."

Derrick was shocked when the handful of customers inside the shop stood up and gave him a round of applause. He was also surprised at how fast the news traveled—the event at the park had only been eight hours ago. A slight flush rushed up his neck to his cheeks. He removed his hat and made a little bow to show his appreciation.

"Thank you, Amy. I'll take my normal black coffee and a Bear Claw. That's to go." Derrick walked up to the counter and thought about his time in Lakeview since he returned. After being gone for so many years, he wasn't sure what he had expected, but it was starting to feel like home—a place where he could put down roots, maybe get married, and start a family. *Wow, where had that thought come from?*

Amy noticed Derrick was lost in thought, so she quietly called his name, "Chief Williams, your order is ready."

Hearing his name got his attention. Derrick looked up to see Amy holding out a cup of steaming coffee and a white bag. He reached for his wallet, but Amy said, "Remember, it's on the house. You deserve it. I hope you enjoy brunch at the Inn later this morning. Sunday brunch at the inn will be a thousand times more delicious than that Bear Claw. Enjoy your day, Chief." With that, Amy returned to the customers waiting to be served.

Is there anything Amy doesn't know? It's true what they say about small towns. News travels faster than the speed of sound. He'd keep that in mind if he needed background information on a case in the future.

Derrick walked outside, intending to head for his car, but it was such a beautiful morning he couldn't resist sitting on one of the benches along Main Street while he ate his breakfast. The sun had moved higher in the sky, casting a yellowish halo on the church steeple at the end of the street. It also launched a gorgeous glow on the baskets hanging at the north end of Main Street. Once again, he appreciated the beautification program in which the town invested.

Finishing his breakfast, he returned to his car, checked for any new calls he needed to respond to, and drove slowly down the street.

Since it was Sunday, the parking meters were turned off. It was the one concession the Town Council had agreed to when they installed them—no meters on Sundays. The equipment was programmed to place a white flag in the window of all meters containing a short note indicating Sundays were free, courtesy of the Town Council.

Derrick saw the town maintenance crew was already hard at work, emptying the trash barrels, sweeping the streets, and watering the plants. He knew the overtime was a bone of contention with some council members, but he also took pride in how nice the Main Street area looked, even on a Sunday.

A flash of red caught his attention. He noticed that one of the meters had a red flag showing in the window. He didn't think much about it until he saw another red flag in the window of a parking meter further along the street. Considering this was Sunday, all meters should be showing a white flag. Thinking about the recent complaints about the meters, he decided to park his car and walk along the street where he saw the red flags.

After walking further along the street, he noticed puddles of water at the base of every meter with a red flag. He checked the flag color on meters without water near their base, and they were all white, as expected.

It hit him like a ton of bricks. Was the water flowing from the hanging flowerpots into the electronic parking meters, causing them to malfunction? Could that be the issue? But wait, why wouldn't rain also cause them to malfunction?

Derrick jumped back in his car and drove to the south end of the street, closer to the police station and town hall. Fewer complaints were coming from this end of the street versus the northern end, closer to the shops. He wanted to determine what was different on the street's southern end. He noticed that due to the reserved parking for the police and town officials, there were fewer parking meters on this end of the street. That might account for fewer tickets on the southern part of the street, but he wasn't sure.

Getting back out of his car, he walked along the street and saw a repeat of what he'd noticed near The Perk. The meters under the hanging baskets all showed the red 'time-expired' flags.

Derrick scratched his head and headed back to his office. He had some paperwork to finish before heading to the inn. If he could figure this mystery out, he hoped Trish would show her appreciation with another one of those passionate kisses. He looked at his watch. He had two hours to solve the mystery.

Derrick headed out of town. He stopped briefly at his office and looked up the address of Mark Brooks, who headed up the Lakeview Maintenance Department. It was only a ten-minute drive.

When he arrived, the Brooks family was pulling into their driveway.

Seeing the Chief of Police in their driveway made Mrs. Brooks comment to her husband, "This can't be good news.

Please find out what is going on while I hurry the kids into the house. If it's bad news, I'd rather they hear it from us."

It was a common concern when a police officer unexpectedly showed up at someone's house. People always jumped to the worst-case scenario.

Derrick got out of his car, walked over to Mark Brooks and the two men shook hands. Mark was on the Town Council and the two would see each other at meetings, so they were familiar with each other and their roles within the town.

Derrick spoke first. "I'm sorry to bother you on Sunday, but I have one quick question. It may sound a bit odd, but it's important. Is the liquid your team uses to water the hanging baskets along Main Street plain water, or do you add other ingredients?"

If Derrick thought Mr. Brooks was confused when he came home to find a police car in his driveway, the new curious look on his face was comical.

"I'm confused about what you're asking me. Let me see if I have this straight. You show up at my home on a Sunday and want me to clarify what we use to water the hanging baskets on Main Street. Do I have that correct?"

Derrick could understand the confusion, but the sooner the question was answered, the sooner he could get to brunch at the inn.

"Yes, that's correct," Derrick responded, trying not to sound frustrated.

After pausing to consider his response, Mr. Brooks finally said, "We use a mixture of ninety percent water, and the other nine percent is a combination of a biocide to inhibit the growth of fungi and an acidifier to lower the acidity of our local water. The last percent is a mixture of Epsom salt and baking soda. The local university's horticulture department helped us design the specific combination several years ago, and as you can see, our hanging baskets benefit from the cocktail. But I'm still a bit confused. Why are you asking about what we use to water the hanging baskets?"

"Epsom salt and baking soda? These would create a bit of a gritty substance, wouldn't they?"

"I've never given it any thought, but I believe you would be correct. Again, why are you asking these odd questions?"

"You may find this hard to believe, but I think the watering cocktail, as you call it, runs over the sides of the baskets and into the new parking meters, causing them to malfunction. Rainwater doesn't seem to bother the equipment, but the gritty mixture does. I believe this is causing all the ruckus about the 'time-expired' complaints in town."

After several moments of silence, Mr. Brooks replied, "Yes, I can see how the gritty substance could potentially cause some type of malfunction. And if it only happens on the meters under the baskets, that would seem to prove your observation. My only question is, what do we do about it? The town paid a fortune to have those baskets hung on the street poles, and the meters have been located under them for years."

Derrick shook his head. "I'm not sure. I'll check with the Mayor tomorrow and have them work with the firm that made the meters to see if there are alternatives to moving them or relocating the hanging baskets. Again, I'm sorry to interrupt your Sunday. I'm sure we'll see each other this week."

Derrick tipped his hat when Mrs. Brooks joined them on the driveway. She had heard the end of the conversation and was trying not to laugh. She turned to her husband, "Dear, I haven't had a chance to tell you yet, but yesterday afternoon, I stopped at The Perk to get a quick coffee, and when I came out, I had a ticket on my window. It said 'time-expired' as the reason. I'm glad you two figured this out so I won't have to pay the fine and get a lecture from you about how I lose track of time when I'm in town shopping." With that comment, she turned around and went back into the house.

The two men shook hands again, and Derrick headed to his cruiser. Looking at his watch, he saw that he needed to hurry so he had time to run home and change out of his uniform. Since the staff at the inn didn't eat until after the official brunch was over, he had enough time to change, send an email to the Mayor, and get to the inn.

He backed out of the driveway, turned the radio on, heard one of his favorite songs about lazy Sundays, and turned up the volume. About halfway to his house, he realized he was singing along with the radio. He was slightly lighthearted and happy. He wasn't sure if potentially solving one of the town's big mysteries or the fact that he was spending the rest of the day with Trish was the reason behind his mood, but he was leaning toward the possibility of having another make-out session with her.

He picked up his speed, feeling the need to hurry and get home, but quickly reduced it. He didn't want people to see him speeding and think he felt above the law. He always tried to set an excellent example for others, so he slowed down, but in his mind, he was itching to get to the inn.

CHAPTER TWENTY-FOUR

Trish walked into the kitchen and found Cassidy, Amanda, and Peter busy putting the final touches on the brunch. She noticed Cassidy sitting at a table with her feet on a low stool. That was good to see, she wouldn't have to scold her for overdoing it.

The kitchen smelled wonderful. The elaborate menu added to the popularity of the meal with both the guests of the inn and residents of Lakeview. The menu changed slightly based on the season and the availability of fresh ingredients. Today's menu included Crab Cake Sliders, Norwegian Smoked Sea Trout, a made-to-order omelet station, a carving station with New York Strip and Rack of Lamb, a variety of veggies, bread, a tower of sweets, and of course, Peter's famous homemade cinnamon buns.

Trish heard a grumbling sound and realized it was her stomach. The grumbling was so loud that Cassidy heard it and started to laugh. "Maybe you should sneak a bite of something to eat so our guests don't hear that rumble. We have a full dining room for the next four hours, so put on your comfy shoes, grab a quick bite, and get ready for the fun."

"No one needs to ask me twice. My mouth is watering for a Crab Cake Slider. Once I finish it, I'll go into the dining room and help the extra staff you bring in on Sundays. Most of them are regular workers, but I noticed two new servers. Fingers crossed, they don't spill anything today."

Trish felt wistful all of a sudden. "I remember when you started offering brunch to others beyond those staying at the inn. You hired some high school kids, and they spilled the entire soup terrine all over the dessert table. What a mess. It's a wonder the customers who experienced that day ever returned, but I see several of them again today. Peter's cooking is the magic key that brings them back, again and again."

Peter spoke up, adding, "It's also the sweet treats Amanda has perfected over time. She's become an accomplished pastry chef. That course she took last year at the famous Culinary Institute of America was worth every penny of the cost. Luckily, I'm frequently the recipient of her experimentation.

Wait until you taste today's dessert special. It's called Death by Chocolate. It's a Molten Chocolate Cupcake. It starts with a chocolate cake base, flowing dark chocolate in the center, chocolate buttercream icing, and shaved chocolate on the top. I think each serving has about a thousand calories. I've had two this week as Amanda perfected the right temperature to set on the serving station to keep the chocolate centers liquid without making the buttercream icing melt. I think you'll be amazed at the results. You'll have to try one, that is, if there are any left when we sit down to eat after the brunch is closed."

"I'll head out to the dining room now. If you need me, don't hesitate to let me know," and Trish headed out of the kitchen.

The next few hours were hectic but enjoyable. It was good to see so many local Lakeview residents. It also gave Trish time to say hello to some of her frequent customers from the shop and to connect with friends.

By three o'clock, Trish wished she'd taken Cassidy's advice and worn sneakers. The heeled sandals looked cute with her navy blue blazer and slacks, but they were no longer cute after she had run around for four hours.

As the last of their guests were leaving and the crew was cleaning up the dining room, Trish took a quick break to go to her apartment in the back of the inn to freshen up and change her shoes. She wanted to look nice for Derrick, but hopefully, he would overlook her bright pink sneakers.

On her way back to the kitchen, she took a minute to look out the large front window and couldn't help but be amazed at the colors she saw. Between the beautiful gardens of the inn, the trees around the lake, and the sun glistening off the water, the colors ran the gamut of the color palette. The overall impact was stunning. It took her breath away.

Continuing to gaze out the window, she noticed that Derrick's car wasn't in the parking lot. There was always the chance that he'd get called away for an emergency. She needed to check her cell phone, which she had left in her room, to see if he had left her a message. If he couldn't make it today, she'd be disappointed.

Recently, Trish knew her feelings for Derrick were growing deeper. Did he feel the same? Things seemed to be moving fast. Maybe some of their former feelings were kicking in, but it was more than that. This was a much more mature feeling. Was it lust? Was it love? She couldn't clearly put a title on it yet, but she knew her heart pounded faster when she was in his arms. Her entire body tingled when he kissed her.

Derrick wasn't the high school jock anymore. He was a more complex version of the boy who left Lakeview many years ago. He'd seen sadness, hurt, pain, and unbelievable injustice. All of this was a recipe that added up to a harder shell and a maturity about doing the right thing. Trish admired the grown-up Derrick. He had been an adorable teenager, but he was an even sexier man.

Trish knew her friends would always support her, but first, she needed to ensure they got to know the grown-up version of Derrick. Her friends were her family, and if their relationship continued to move forward as she hoped it would, she desperately wanted their full approval.

When she returned to the dining room, Trish was surprised when she saw Cassidy's mother and stepfather. Kate had been a widow for many years and then met Duncan Moore. They had a whirlwind courtship and married. Duncan was a father figure to Cassidy and her younger sister, Adelaide. Kate called Duncan her second Prince Charming.

Kate was always dressed perfectly, and today was no different. She mainly wore designer brands, but today, Trish was thrilled to see Kate wearing clothes from her new line. She wasn't even aware Kate had been at Crystal Lake Gifts since she started selling Lakeview Designs. Kate wore a tailored red blazer, white silk shell, dark navy slacks, and the perfect amount of jewelry to complete her outfit.

Everyone was already seated, with two empty seats between Cassidy and Amanda. Everyone was talking, and Trish heard someone filling Kate in on the excitement from the Fourth of July Picnic and how Derrick and Trish delivered little Elijah Foster.

Trish teased Cassidy about not waiting until the last minute to leave for the hospital, or she and Derrick would be delivering her baby in the backseat of his police car.

Cassidy shivered at the thought. She was committed to leaving for the hospital at the appropriate time to avoid an emergency and keep her family happy. Her mother worked hard to get funding for the new Neonatal Unit at the hospital. Cassidy intended to take advantage of the luxurious accommodations, which included the option for a relaxing massage and bath before being discharged. What a fantastic way to make a new mother feel special before heading home.

Everyone looked up as Derrick walked into the room. Introductions were made, and Trish and Derrick took their seats between Cassidy and Amanda.

Kate immediately turned to Derrick. "I'm so glad you and Trish were there to help little Elijah into the world. Dr. Foster was so appreciative. He's a proud father who always shows me pictures of his family. They seem to be settling in nicely in Lakeview.

We are so fortunate that he opted to join our community hospital versus one of those larger city hospitals. Especially now that Cassidy and Jack are expecting, I think I'll sleep better at night knowing they have a world-class hospital less than fifteen minutes away from their cottage."

Derrick was used to getting thanks for his work, especially in helping with difficult situations, his afterschool work with the at-risk kids, saving a cat from the lake, or even helping accident victims until the EMT units arrived, but in this more intimate setting, he seemed embarrassed to get such praise.

"I was trained in emergency deliveries, and with Trish there to help me and a second-time mother, it all went by the textbooks. On the other hand, I wasn't sure who was happier to see Dr. Foster arrive, Leah Foster or me. I'm so glad mother and baby are doing fine."

Derrick reached for Trish's hand under the table and opted not to share that she came close to fainting after the delivery. That could be their little secret.

Trish immediately felt tingles run up her arm as Derrick held her hand. Without meaning to, her body leaned slightly to her right to reduce the distance between her and Derrick. For a split second, she forgot where they were. She turned her face toward Derrick, slightly opening her lips, sending a subtle message that she was asking for a kiss, but she heard Jack asking everyone to bow their heads for a blessing of the food, family, and friends gathered at the table on this glorious Sunday.

Trish realized she had almost made a fool of herself. Kissing someone at Sunday brunch wasn't anything she ever thought she'd do. She needed to get her emotions under control. Did Derrick know what she was thinking?

With their heads bowed and eyes closed, Trish couldn't read his facial expression, but she was comforted when Derrick lightly squeezed her hand. It gave her a calming feeling. Or at least she had felt calmer, until Derrick started rubbing his thumb across the palm of her hand. The slow circular motion caused chills to run up her arms, yet heat spread throughout the rest of her body. She could feel her neck and cheeks burning.

As soon as the prayer was over and everyone started passing the food, Trish stood up and removed her blazer. She needed to cool off and put some space between her and Derrick before she did something stupid. She walked across the room and hung her jacket on a hook near the door.

Before returning to her seat, she walked over to the dessert table and put a variety of items on a tray so the group could pick which one they wanted to eat. It also gave her time to cool down.

Sitting back down at the table, she moved her chair closer to Cassidy. She needed a little breathing room from Derrick right now. But all bets were off for later this evening.

CHAPTER TWENTY-FIVE

Once brunch was wrapped up, the group decided to have their after-dinner, or in this case, after-brunch drinks, outside on the porch. It was such a glorious day, and as the afternoon turned into early evening, the sun was lower in the sky and the sparkle on the lake was even more breathtaking.

From the porch, Trish could smell the flowers from the manicured flowerbeds that ran along the walkway to the lake and around the inn. Although the air could sometimes feel like a sauna in July, an overnight rain shower had lowered the humidity and the temperatures while watering the gardens. It would be a comfortable evening for a walk.

"Anyone want to walk along the lake?" Amanda asked.

Before anyone could respond, Trish spoke up. "I was hoping to hear about your upcoming trip to Las Vegas. I know you and Peter want to make a trip before Cassidy and Jack's baby is born, and we've lined up extra help at the inn. Are you still planning on leaving next week? What do you plan to do while you're there? I hope we don't have to send you money if you bet too much at the casinos."

Trish thought she had seen a quick look pass between Peter and Amanda, but it was gone so quickly she couldn't be sure. "What are you two up to?" Trish asked.

Peter stood up from his chair and moved closer to Amanda. "We planned a quiet trip. After our hectic schedules here at the inn and our volunteer work in Lakeview, along with Amanda helping at Crystal Lake Gifts, we've been running non-stop. It's time for a quiet week in a luxury hotel suite. We plan to order lots of room service and let someone else cook for us.

"Of course, I used some of my connections in the restaurant world to get us seats at the Chef's Table at Restaurant Guy Savoy. They feature classic French cuisine but with a modern twist. When we're at Caesar's for dinner, we plan to see a show and maybe throw a few bucks away at the slots, but mainly, we want to relax by the pool and get a nice tan."

Trish noticed that Amanda didn't add anything to Peter's comments. That was odd. She planned to check in later with Amanda to be sure everything was okay between her and Peter. They seemed to be getting more and more serious lately, and she hoped nothing was wrong.

Kate and Duncan said their goodbyes and headed home. "We have an early morning tomorrow. Duncan needs to be at his headquarters in New York City for the week and asked me to join him. I don't typically travel with him when it's business, but he reminded me I could do some shopping for a special upcoming event. Since baby clothes don't take up much room in my luggage, I plan on having a blast at the designer baby shops in the city."

Without anyone noticing it, Cassidy had shut her eyes and was already lightly snoring.

Kate leaned over and lightly kissed Cassidy on the cheek. She turned to speak to Jack, "Please ask Cassidy to check in with me every day, or else I'll worry." Jack hugged his mother-in-law, shook hands with Duncan, and walked them to the front door.

When Jack returned, he walked over to his wife and whispered in her ear, "Mrs. Burnett, it's time to go home so you can get some rest." Jack leaned over and helped Cassidy get out of the Adirondack chair.

"I'm so sorry, gang. I didn't mean to fall asleep. It seems to be happening a lot these days. Jack and I should head home, but not before I hear about Peter and Amanda's plans to visit Vegas next week."

The group broke out in laughter. "What did I say?" Looking toward Amanda, Cassidy asked if they were still going.

Jack put his arm around his wife. "Dear, I'll fill you in on our way home. It seems you slept through the update."

"Oh my. I'm so sorry. We better be going before I fall asleep again. It was a wonderful day. I'll see most of you tomorrow."

As Jack and Cassidy headed to their car, Amanda and Trish agreed they hoped they could get Cassidy to stop working at the inn soon. She had been so tired lately, and her doctor only gave her another two weeks to work.

The group waved as Jack and Cassidy drove away. They remained silent, watching the sun sink further down in the sky.

Derrick broke the silence, "I heard the town still sponsors the annual Labor Day picnic and parade, and the inn hosts the fireworks display. It sounds wonderful, but we will be busy handling traffic, partygoers, floats, and fireworks. Do you ever get to take off on a holiday? I know the small police force is expected to work the holidays, but do the three of you also work every holiday?"

Peter responded, "Yep. Amanda, Cassidy, and Trish have always volunteered in some capacity during special holiday events, and when I moved here, I got roped in, and then Jack and now you."

Amanda was quick to speak up, "Roped in? If I recall, you were the one who talked Cassidy into sponsoring the fireworks. You said it was a fantastic marketing campaign, and it was easier to feed people here than drag everything to the park."

"That's true. We all love the sense of community in Lakeview, so we happily volunteer."

Derrick appeared thoughtful for a second. "Based on the unplanned excitement of the Fourth of July picnic, let's hope we don't have another mom go into unexpected labor on Labor Day." The others chuckled at his weak attempt at a joke. "We'd all be happier if Cassidy got to the hospital in plenty of time for her delivery. Let's keep an eye on her and be sure she doesn't wait until the last minute to head to Lakeview Hospital."

"Amen to that," Trish said.

It was gorgeous this time of day as the sun lowered in the sky and turned a deeper blue. Trish, Derrick, Amanda, and Peter decided to take a walk along the lake. The group talked about their upcoming vacation plans but mainly walked quietly, enjoying the views.

Thirty minutes later, Peter and Amanda returned to the inn to do a bit of prep for the next day. Derrick and Trish decided to linger along the lake a little longer.

"I love being by the lake right before the sun sets. It's so peaceful. It feels like we are the only ones here." Trish gazed at the horizon.

Derrick looked around and realized they were actually alone, so he took full advantage of the situation. Stepping closer to Trish, he put his hands on each side of her tiny waist and turned her toward him. He wanted to take it slow, but once he saw the desire in her large blue eyes, he quickly pulled her to his chest and claimed her lips. Running his hands through her hair, he drew her even closer. The kisses were passionate, and both were breathing hard. When hands started to roam, Trish jumped back to regain her composure.

"I think we are getting a little bit carried away in making out in public, and there is a clear view of us from the inn." With a little giggle, Trish quietly said, "We are acting like teenagers."

"I'm sure glad I'm not a teenager," Derrick said softly. "I know exactly what I want to do right now, but I agree a public place isn't appropriate. Honestly, Trish, it's getting harder for me to restrain myself. I know this is happening faster than we intended."

Trish was caught off guard. Within the last few weeks, she also realized she had feelings for Derrick, but she didn't think he was in the same place as she was. "I know whenever we're together, I can't think straight, my heart rate goes up, and my hands get clammy."

"I feel the same way." Derrick pulled her back into his arms, sweetly kissed her lips again, and moved down to her neck, but he stopped himself. "I don't want to do something stupid, so let's finish our walk and cool off."

Derrick led Trish back up the walkway to the inn. At the door, he planted a light kiss on her lips, said goodnight, and walked down toward his car.

Trish stood at the door, still breathless. She touched her fingers to her lips, which were still warm from his last kiss. Even though the evening air had cooled off, Trish felt warm all over, like she was wrapped in a cozy quilt.

CHAPTER TWENTY-SIX

"I pronounce you husband and wife. You can kiss the bride." Peter could hear the words but could hardly believe he and Amanda had eloped in Las Vegas. Looking down at her left hand and seeing the ruby ring he placed on her finger seemed to seal the deal.

"Well, Mrs. Cooper, Congratulations." Peter pulled Amanda into a warm hug and gave her a romantic kiss. The kiss continued until he heard the officiant clear his throat, a sign that the newlyweds should get a room.

Speaking of rooms, with Peter's connections, he had been able to book the honeymoon suite and arranged for a lavish five-course meal to be served in their room. The suite was gorgeous, and the lights of the Vegas strip glittered through the ceiling-to-floor windows.

Upon arriving at their room and opening the door, the delicious smell of fresh steamed lobster and other foods greeted them.

Walking over to the elegantly decorated table, Amanda saw tall, tapered candles flickering and setting off the gleaming white china. She also noticed a salad with fresh pears, filet mignon, lobster tails with melted butter, baked potatoes, and steamed kale in a cream sauce. Looking over at another small table, she saw a two-tier wedding cake.

"It's wonderful. The meal looks delicious, and the wedding cake is beautiful. You did a fabulous job of organizing everything. I couldn't be happier, and it's exactly what I wanted."

Peter looked at his new bride. "When you agreed to elope, I worried you were giving up a big fancy wedding. With your family's connections in the international business arena, there wasn't any way you could have had the small, intimate wedding you said you dreamed of, but still, are you sure you're okay with eloping? Won't Trish and Cassidy be upset with you?"

"My parents and close friends might be surprised by our eloping, but I also think they'll be happy for us. But remember, we don't plan to tell anyone until after Cassidy has her baby. She is due any time now, and we don't want to steal the limelight from her special event. Besides, I think keeping our little secret to ourselves for a few more weeks will be romantic."

"I guess the old saying is true—what happens in Vegas stays in Vegas," Peter chuckled. "I'll respect your wishes, but it's a good thing we already live together because there are some activities I can't refrain from." Peter pulled his wife into his arms, and after a round of kisses that left them both breathless, dinner was forgotten. Peter scooped Amanda into his arms and carried her into the large bedroom.

Several hours later, the couple emerged from the bedroom. They were famished, but after looking at the cold food sitting in congealed butter, they decided to order from the twenty-four-hour room service.

"Hello. Can I have two cheeseburgers, two orders of fries, and two chocolate milkshakes delivered to the honeymoon suite, please?" Amanda heard Peter order their dinner, and she sadly placed the domes back on the dried-out steak.

"Our food will be here in fifteen minutes. If you can keep your hands off me that long, we'll finally get to eat."

Amanda couldn't help but laugh. This entire weekend had been surreal, but she couldn't be happier. "Okay, Mr. Cooper, I'll stay on this side of the room, and you stay on the far side of the room until our food is delivered. That will help us keep our hands to ourselves."

Peter stood still for about two seconds before he ran across the room, grabbed Amanda, and scooped her up again, but this time he settled for the couch. Hot passion emanated from the couple. Amanda's dressing gown slid to the floor, and things started to heat up, but they were interrupted by the doorbell.

"I guess we better eat our food this time. There's still an entire week for us to cuddle up and make mad, passionate love for hours. But first, I've got to eat to keep up my strength."

With that, Peter threw a dressing gown to his wife and grabbed the tray from the room service porter.

Their week in Vegas flew by. Before they were ready, it was their last evening in the city of bright lights. The past week had been a flurry of activities. They hiked in Red Rock Canyon, visited Hoover Dam, relaxed by the hotel's pool, attended several shows at various casinos, and thoroughly enjoyed a meal to remember at Restaurant Guy Savoy.

Tonight, their last night in Vegas, they were due to be guests of Coco Diamond, the famous restauranteur. Coco had a chain of high-end restaurants sprinkled across the globe. She and Peter had crossed paths several years earlier when Peter was the head chef at a famous ski lodge. Coco had heard through the grapevine he was in town and invited them to her private table for dinner.

"I know Coco is famous, and I should be thrilled we are invited to join her for dinner, but I'd much prefer to spend a quiet night with my new hubby," Amanda said. "We fly home tomorrow, and I wanted to indulge in a bubble bath with you. It will be too late when we get back to the hotel after dinner, and honestly, I'm already tired, so by later tonight, I'll be asleep on my feet. Do we have to go?"

"My sweet Amanda. Of course, we don't have to go if you truly don't want to join Coco. But I don't want to offend her, and it's always good to have a connection like her in my corner. Are you too tired to go, or is it something else?"

"I'm tired, but I don't know what it is exactly. I don't like how she sent us several lavish gifts and asked us to join her for dinner at the last minute. It feels like she has an ulterior motive. Could she want something from you? Maybe she is looking for a new private chef. I love our life and don't want anyone rocking the boat." Amanda pushed out her bottom lip to show she was pouting.

"If we are going to be on time for dinner, we need to leave in an hour. I'll leave the final decision to you. If you truly don't want to go to dinner, I'll call her now."

Amanda thought about it briefly but realized Peter was right. They couldn't decline, especially this late. "Okay, I guess we'll go. I've already done my hair and makeup and only have to get dressed."

Amanda turned around and headed toward the bedroom. When she heard Peter call her name, she stopped and turned around.

"While you're getting dressed, I'd appreciate it if you also put on one more thing."

"I already showed you the dress I was wearing to dinner. What else could you want me to put on?" Amanda looked confused.

Peter gave her one of his endearing smiles and said, "Be sure to put on your smile. When you smile, the whole world lights up. No more pouting. Okay?"

As Amanda turned back toward the bedroom, she called over her shoulder, "No promises, Mr. Cooper."

Five hours later, Peter and Amanda walked back into their honeymoon suite. Peter was quiet, and Amanda was unsettled. Amanda was the first to speak, "Peter, are you okay? You were quiet on the ride back to our hotel. What are you thinking?"

"Coco's offer came out of nowhere. I barely know her. Why would she offer me the head chef role at her new restaurant in New York City?"

"It's simple, she knows you're the best. Coco said she has high hopes for the new restaurant, and putting you in the head spot would ensure Michelin stars right from the start. You may have left the bright lights to live a simpler life in Lakeview, but your reputation still follows you." Amanda curled up on the sofa in their sitting room. "I know our life is mapped out in Maine, but I never want to stand in your way. If you want us to move to New York City, I'm prepared to support your dreams and move."

"Amanda, it's not that simple. We've made a life together in Maine. I'm the chef for the inn, and we've built the inn's reputation around our hospitality and high-end food. Cassidy gave me a job when I was floundering to find my way. I owe her some loyalty."

Amanda carefully choose her next words, "Yes, you did owe her for a while, but Cassidy would be the first to tell you to follow your dreams. If we both leave, there would be a bigger gap. Maybe you can go to New York and get the project started, and I can join you later. It's only a four or five-hour drive. I can split my time until Cassidy and Jack settle down with the baby, and she can find and train new staff. We can find a solution that works for all of us."

"I need time to think about this. It's a major decision. Our five-hour flight home tomorrow will give me plenty of time to weigh the pros and cons. Let's leave it alone for now."

Peter walked over to his new bride and pulled her into a sweet kiss, which turned into a passionate kiss, which turned into clothes flying, dimmed lights, and a bedroom door slamming shut.

CHAPTER TWENTY-SEVEN

It was midnight when Peter and Amanda got to the inn. Their flight had been delayed, and the Uber from Portland Airport to Lakeview was a no-show, so they had to book another car.

The trip, which started as a wonderful adventure, had become more serious once Coco made the offer to Peter. The newlyweds were quiet on the car ride home.

Amanda wanted to give Peter all the time he needed to respond to Coco's offer. While she had been looking forward to their married life in Lakeview, she also wanted to support her new husband. They decided to keep their elopement a secret for a few weeks, which added another complexity to their decision about Peter's career.

Looking down at the beautiful ruby ring Peter had given her, Amanda reminded herself she needed to slip the ring off her finger and keep it in her jewelry box until they announced their marriage. If she kept it on her finger, there was no way Trish and Cassidy wouldn't notice the ring and start asking questions.

Peter and Amanda agreed not to mention their elopement and Coco's offer until they understood better what they planned to do. They didn't want to get everyone churned up if they decided not to stay at the inn, especially with Cassidy getting closer to her due date.

"It feels so good to be home," Amanda said as they got into bed. "I'm so tired I could sleep for a week. We were busy every day of our vacation. I'm glad we thought ahead and had the temp chef stay an extra day. That will allow us time to settle back in."

"I agree. I fell asleep in the Uber," Peter said as he tried to hold back a big yawn. "I'm looking forward to a good night's sleep, and I want to check out my kitchen tomorrow afternoon to ensure everything is in order. I hope it's not a big mess." He turned over to kiss his wife goodnight, only to find she was already asleep.

Peter knew he would be awake for several hours playing out the possible scenarios. Making the wrong decision could ruin their relationship, create contention with their friends, and impact his reputation. He needed to be fully confident in the choice he made.

As much as Peter wanted to keep playing scenarios through his mind, his body was too physically exhausted to join his brain in the problem-solving exercise, and within two minutes, he was also fast asleep.

Time flew by, and before it seemed real, the town was gearing up for the Labor Day festivities. The final weeks of summer were going fast, and in typical Maine style, it was prime vacation time. Every inn, hotel, and restaurant was packed. No vacancy signs were everywhere, both on the cute old-fashioned signs in front yards, and the electronic versions online. Main Street was a beehive of activity, including Crystal Lake Gifts.

Sales were beyond expectations at the store, which was good and bad. The extra sales helped push the store over its forecast. On the other hand, keeping the shelves stocked was a challenge. Trish and Sarah came in early to stock shelves and keep the store open late on Wednesday and Friday nights.

They still had thirty minutes before they opened the store and were done stocking the shelves for the day. Trish walked over to where Sarah had rearranged a shelf. "Wow!" Trish said, "Can you believe we've already sold out of those hand-made quilts? I thought we had enough to last us through fall, the typical time of year we sell the most. A woman from Maryland bought the last six we had on the shelf. She was adding them to her large collection at home. When I asked her how many quilts were in her collection, she laughed and said she had too many to count. As much as I love handmade quilts, I don't think I've ever bought six at one time. She said the quality was fabulous, and she couldn't resist. I'm glad her husband was with her to lug them to their car."

Sarah moved other merchandise around to cover the empty space on the shelf, picked up the plastic wrapping she removed from the new items, and turned to Trish, "I think we have everything stocked. Let's grab a cup of coffee before we open the doors."

Trish and Sarah headed to the breakroom. Sarah sat down to wait for Trish to get her coffee first.

As Trish reached for her favorite K-cup, her phone rang. Reaching into her pocket to remove her phone, she saw it was Derrick.

"Hello, Derrick. It's so good to hear your voice. I only have a minute. What's up?"

"I know you'll be busy today. The sidewalks in town are already crowded with tourists. I need a couple of minutes to speak with you later. Will you be able to get away for lunch?"

Trish thought about the staff coming in today, but even with extra help, she wasn't comfortable taking time away from the shop. "I don't think that will work today. Maybe we can grab dinner after the shop closes today."

"I have a Labor Day planning meeting at six tonight with the Mayor, so that won't work. If we don't connect today, let's meet early tomorrow at The Perk. Say around seven? I have something interesting to discuss with you. Will that work for you?"

"Now you've piqued my curiosity. Tell me what you want to discuss now, or it will drive me crazy all day."

"Nope. Let's see how things play out today, and if nothing works, I'll meet you outside The Perk at seven in the morning. If you get there before me, grab your coffee, sit outside, and enjoy the breathtaking beauty of the flowering baskets flowing down Main Street. All too soon, they will be gone for the season."

Trish still wondered what was up, and she thought it was a little odd Derrick mentioned the hanging baskets on

Main Street. She couldn't remember him ever commenting on how beautiful the flowers were in the past. But she knew she'd be too busy today to meet with him, so she was happy they had a backup plan for tomorrow morning. "Okay, if I don't see you later today, I'll meet you at The Perk at seven sharp." Trish's conversation was cut short when she heard her name called and a reminder from Sarah that it was time to open the shop.

As it turned out, the day was hectic and Trish forgot Derrick wanted to talk to her. The shop was packed all day, and after closing, she and Sarah stayed to restock. As much as she was over the moon about the success of the expanded shop, there were days when she knew she'd soon have to make serious decisions about hiring a full-time manager and more staff. Right now, she wanted to return to the inn for dinner—a quick walk around the lake and a long bubble bath before bed.

The following day, Trish arrived at The Perk a little before seven, grabbed her coffee, and went outside to sit on the bench in front of the coffee shop. She didn't see Derrick's car and thought maybe he got called away on police business.

While she waited, she noticed the Lakeview Maintenance team was out in full force, emptying the trashcans and sweeping up debris from the sidewalk, and someone was watering the beautiful hanging baskets. She was so proud of their little town and the support they got from the Town Council and Merchants Association to keep the town clean and attractive.

She was so engrossed in watching the young man wheel the water tank down the street and stop every few feet to water the baskets she failed to notice Derrick had already been inside The Perk, got his coffee, and was standing beside the bench.

"Good Morning, Sweetheart," Derrick said as he sat beside Trish.

Trish jumped and smiled when she realized Derrick was sitting beside her. "Good Morning to you also, but I didn't see you coming, so you scared me."

"Can I get a good morning kiss?" Derrick teased her, knowing she would say no since it was a busy spot at this time of day.

"Not in public on the Main Street sidewalk, at seven am no less. I'm a reputable businesswoman in this town. What would people think?"

Derrick hesitated for a second, lowered his voice, and responded, "They might think we are interested in each other."

Trish stared at Derrick. She was surprised to hear him say he was interested in her, which caught her off guard.

Derrick continued. "I've been resistant to let my feelings take over. I know you said you had feelings for me the other day at the lake, but I'm not in a rush to push our relationship along faster than what you're comfortable with. I'm in this for the long haul and not going anywhere."

Trish turned to face Derrick. "I need some time to get used to the change in our relationship. My feelings grew quickly, or maybe they were always there, but I only recently realized that I can't deny how I feel."

Trish quickly looked around to see if anyone was watching them. When she thought the coast was clear, she leaned over and touched her lips to Derrick's. When she tried to pull back, Derrick put his arms around her back and leaned in for a passionate kiss. The kiss went on until Trish came to her senses and wiggled out of his arms.

"It's not that I don't enjoy your kisses. I'm not as comfortable with public displays of affection as you seem to be. Maybe we should analyze your history while you were away from Lakeview and determine why that is."

Derrick's smile slipped from his face, and he became serious, "Trish, the years I was away from Lakeview and away from you were not the best years of my life."

Trish held her breath, not sure if she wanted to hear about his past, but he continued.

"I think I took after my old man, who sadly became a drunk after my mom kicked him out. She was left with the mess he created and a thirteen-year-old son who was confused and unsure of how a man should act."

I can relate, Trish thought, remembering her own sad history with her parents and feeling like an orphan. She nodded for him to go on.

"That's why I took your decision to go with another guy to the prom instead of me really hard. I've always had a problem with rejection I guess."

"I did feel bad about that, but I apologized and it was a long time ago," Trish offered.

"I know, but then it went from bad to worse. I fell in love with a woman who stole my heart." Derrick hung his head.

Trish suddenly felt like she couldn't breathe, like she'd been punched in the gut. But still, she remained silent.

"I was a new police officer in New York City, and she was a beautiful actress getting started on Broadway. Her star started to rise, and she got a taste of what it felt like to be famous. We'd go to cast parties and dining engagements, and she was always the center of attention. Meanwhile, I felt like a dog hanging on a leash. So, I stopped going with her to all the fancy parties and started to pick up extra shifts at work. And that's when it happened."

Trish looked at him expectantly. "What?"

"I caught her with another man in our bed when I got off duty earlier than expected one night. I was enraged and threw both of them out of our apartment. And I proceeded to get wasted. My drunkfest lasted for a week or so, until I came dangerously close to being fired. But thank God for my job, which stopped me from doing something stupid."

Trish watched a tear trickle down his face, and a pang of jealousy stabbed her in the heart. "What was her name?"

"Does it really matter?" Trish nodded yes so Derrick responded. "Her name was Rhonda Jennings."

"The famous actress? You were in love with Rhonda Jennings?" Trish was aghast. She stammered out, "D-do you still l-luh-love her?"

Derrick turned to face her. "No, I don't. It took me a few years to get over her. I was finally able to move on with my life. I need to be perfectly honest with you because I'm falling in love with you."

"Do you still have a drinking problem?"

"No, I wouldn't be the Chief of Police if I did. I got help with better ways to handle my anger and my drinking, which also has helped me to handle the overall pressure of my line of work. It was a win-win for me and my career."

Trish stood up and started pacing in front of the bench. *Maybe I'm a rebound?* She felt her anger rise. She didn't want to ask questions or know any more about his sordid past. She rubbed her arms, feeling the chill of a breeze off the lake wrap around her.

"Derrick, I will have to think about all of this. Right now, it's all too much to get my head around. I think we should take a break for a while..."

Derrick stood to face Trish, his face contorted with emotion. "How can you say that? I was completely honest with you because I trusted you." His radio beeped, and he answered it. "I have to go."

"Fine," Trish said defensively. ""I know my way back alone."

CHAPTER TWENTY-EIGHT

Trish woke up to a text from Derrick asking her to meet him at The Perk. He said he'd never gotten a chance to explain what he'd initially planned to tell her. Her pulse started to race, and the heat moved up her neck to her cheeks.

She was unsure whether this was a good idea, but he said it was important, it wouldn't take long, and it would remain strictly platonic.

When she entered the coffee shop, Derrick was already seated, nursing a coffee. She ordered and paid for it herself, noticing Amy's curious look. Thankfully, none of her other friends were there. Sarah was busy tending the store for her, Cassidy was home resting, and Amanda and Peter were busy at the inn.

They went outside and sat on a bench to drink their coffees and watch the activity on the street, getting lost in their thoughts. Finally, Derrick said, "Are you still interested in hearing why I asked you to meet me here yesterday morning…and again now?"

Trish shrugged.

"I think you'll be interested in finding out what I wanted to share with you."

Her curiosity got the better of her. "Okay, what's up?"

Derrick pointed down the street toward Town Hall. Trish followed where he was pointing and waited for him to explain.

"To make a long story short, I think we've solved the parking meter mystery. Yesterday, I saw you watching the maintenance worker water the hanging baskets. Take a closer look at what is sitting under the baskets."

"I don't understand. What do the hanging baskets have to do with malfunctioning parking meters?"

Derrick understood how crazy this all sounded. He had already worked through it. "Do you see the water trickling from the bottom of the baskets? Look to see where it's going."

Trish stood up to get a better look. Water trickled down from the bottom of the baskets and hit the ground. Looking up the street at the other baskets, she noticed a couple dripping water into the parking meters.

"I see water running into a few of the meters, but what I don't understand is the meters are watertight. Rain doesn't affect them. Are you trying to tell me the water is causing the problem? That doesn't make sense."

Derrick knew it was time to tell her the missing mystery pieces to help her connect the dots. "The difference between the wastewater from the baskets and rain is the water used to water the plants has other chemicals and additives. The combination of those additives makes a gritty substance which is eating away at the layer protecting the internal mechanisms and causing the machines to malfunction.

"I met with Mark Brooks, the head of the Lakeview Maintenance Department, who confirmed the situation. After thoughtful consideration and a month of follow-up calls to the equipment manufacturer, we fully agree the watering of the hanging baskets is causing the malfunction of the new automated parking meters." Derrick paused to let Trish absorb the information.

"I'm shocked. Who figured that out? How did they figure it out?"

"Slow down and let me finish. I sat on this same bench and watched the guys water the baskets one day. After watching the same process several times, I realized excess water was running into the meters. But I still couldn't figure it out because, like you, I know the meters are sealed tight, so the rain is not a problem. Next, I started to examine certain meters placed under the baskets, and I went to see Mark. It all started to come together when he explained that the water used for the baskets contained chemicals and additives. We conducted more research with the meter manufacturer and confirmed the issue.

"I need to update the Town Council, and they can decide how best to handle the situation," Derrick paused to let Trish catch up.

"WOW! That is amazing. You solved the mystery and probably saved the town from a lawsuit or even having to remove the meters until the issue could be resolved. Too many people are getting the 'time-expired' tickets, and there's an uproar at every Council meeting." Trish was genuinely impressed and felt her hardened heart soften a little inside. *Maybe he's not such a bad guy after all.* *Did I make a mistake in judging Derrick based on his past?*

Without thinking, Trish reached over, took Derrick's hand, and kissed him on the cheek. "You're our Lakeview hero."

Trish heard someone clearing their throat and saw Sarah standing behind them.

"Don't let me interrupt you two, but I'm sure you can find a more private place to make out than on the sidewalk on Main Street," Sarah said, trying to stifle a laugh. "What is going on?"

Derrick said, "It's a long story, but we solved the 'time-expired' parking meter problem."

Trish spoke up. "I was showing the Chief of Police my gratitude for solving the 'time-expired' mystery."

Sarah laughed, adding, "I'm not sure if all his constituents are this enthusiastic."

"I certainly hope not," Trish added as she leaned over and placed another quick kiss on his cheek.

CHAPTER TWENTY-NINE

The days leading up to Labor Day were always extremely hectic, and the monthly meeting of the Lakeview Town Council was scheduled for Monday evening, adding to all of the other activities. Trish reviewed the agenda sent to her via email early Monday morning and noticed two ad-hoc topics had been added to the meeting, which typically only lasted ninety minutes. Thirty minutes were set aside to review the plans for the Labor Day weekend coming up in five days, and another fifteen minutes for Chief Williams and Mark Brooks to discuss agenda items listed with vague titles: Meters and Alarms.

After reading the agenda, Trish better understood the odd text message she had received a few minutes earlier. The text was from Derrick, and it hadn't initially made sense, but it got clearer once she read the agenda.

Derrick: ***Good morning, sweetheart.***

Trish: ***Happy Monday to you.***

Derrick: ***I'm tied up all day. I'll see you at the Council Meeting tonight.***

Trish: *I plan to arrive a few minutes early. See you there.*

Derrick: *I can't wait to discuss Chipmunk Bandits and Gritty Meters.*

Trish: *What?*

Derrick: *Read the Council Meeting agenda.*

Trish: *Ok. Give me a minute to pull it up.*

She paused to quickly read the agenda. Trish: *Oh boy, now I understand.*

Trish: *I can't wait until you explain the 'time-expired' meter situation. Even more fun will be the Chipmunk bandits. I especially want to see Mrs. Lester's face.*

Derrick: *Yep. This should be a fun meeting.* (He added the heart emoji)

Trish responded with the heart emoji too. She felt the stirring in her heart he always brought and smiled to herself. *I need to leave the past in the past. We all have history we want to forget, and he was honest with me. That says a lot. Maybe I have been too hard on him. Maybe he's one of the good guys after all.*

As predicted, it was a crazy day in town. Crystal Lake Gifts was packed most of the day, and by five o'clock, Trish couldn't wait to turn the sign on the front door from open to closed. Most days, she stayed open a few extra minutes in case there were any last-minute shoppers, but today, she wanted to straighten up at the store, tally the day's sales, prepare her night deposit, and head out.

The Council Meeting started at six, and she planned to be there early to get a seat in front. This was going to be one of the most interesting meetings ever.

After dropping off the night deposit, she hurried into The Perk to grab a coffee and something to hold her over until after the meeting. She didn't want her tummy rumbling throughout the meeting.

Walking into The Perk, she was surprised to see it was packed. Amy stayed open later during the summer, but typically, by five pm, the shop wasn't busy. Tonight was different, and as she looked across the room, she realized many of the patrons were local business owners. It seemed the Town Council meeting was going to have a full house tonight.

After greeting several of the merchants from along Main Street, she finally got to the counter and waited for someone to take her order.

"Hi, Trish. Sorry for the wait. What can I get you?" Amy asked.

"Wow, you sure are busy for this time of day. Who knew a Council Meeting would drive up your business. I'll take a large light roast coffee and one of those delicious brownies from the display case. That should hold me over until after the meeting."

It only took Amy a couple of minutes to complete Trish's order, and she turned around and handed it to her. "Yep. From the bits of conversations I've overheard, every merchant that's a member of the Council is attending tonight. They seemed intrigued by the agenda. Several merchants hit the hardest by the 'time-expired' issues are fuming since they don't feel like the town has done anything to help ease the customer complaints."

"Without giving any surprises away, I think that problem will be solved tonight, or at least addressed properly." Trish responded and turned to leave, but not before saying goodbye to her friend Amy and telling her they would try to save her a seat up front.

Trish decided walking to the Town Hall would be easier than finding a parking space. The walk took her ten minutes due to the number of people who stopped her to say hello and ask her about the agenda items. Trish apologized for not being able to stop and talk. "We don't have time to stop and chat, or we'll be late, and the Mayor will call us out in front of everyone."

When Trish entered into the meeting room, it was packed. She immediately walked up front when she saw Amanda waving at her. Thank goodness Peter and Amanda saved her a seat.

"Look at this place. I don't recall ever seeing it so crowded," Trish commented. "The two interesting agenda items got everyone's attention."

Before Amanda could respond, they heard the gavel banging on the counter, and the room fell quiet.

The Mayor started the meeting by introducing the council members and reviewing the agenda. He said since there was so much interest in the last two agenda items, he wanted to start with them, so anyone who wanted to leave after that could do so and let the Council get on with the other items.

"I turn the floor over to the Chief of Police, Derrick Williams, and the Head of Maintenance, Mark Brooks. Gentlemen, you have the floor. Please step forward and use the microphone so those in the back can hear you."

Derrick and Mark moved forward, but Derrick took the microphone first.

Derrick hesitated for a second and looked around the room. His eyes fell on Trish, and she felt her heart racing in her chest.

Then he began. "Two issues have been causing the Lakeview rumor mill to go into overtime lately. I'm here to speak about these issues and what our research found. Mr. Brooks is here to support the issue of parking meters. Regrettably, Jack Burnett couldn't be with us tonight to speak about the excessive alarms at Crystal Lake Gifts, but he sent his regards and asked me to relay his findings, which I've validated.

Let's start with the excessive burglar alarms and potential break-ins at Crystal Lake Gifts. Jack Burnett, at the request of Trish Cavanaugh, spent hours reviewing the camera recordings at her shop. Even after Lakeview Electrical had completed an extensive electrical system upgrade, the alarms continued to trip, which caused concern from the surrounding merchants, who feared a burglar was on the loose. That was not the case.

After hours of reviewing recordings, Jack finally identified the bandit. With additional research and patience, the 'bandit' was identified as an Eastern Chipmunk. A family of chipmunks had built a home in the back storage room of the shop, and they had dug a hole behind the electrical panel. As they added more acorns to their hiding place, occasionally, one acorn would push through the insulation behind the panel and allow an acorn to hit the various breakers in the box. Once the breaker was hit, it set off the alarm."

There was so much laughing and talking in the room the Mayor had to hit his gavel and ask for quiet. "Derrick, please continue."

"Once Jack watched this happen several times, with the alarm temporarily turned off so as not to call the police, he and Trish called Tom Spencer from Lakeview Electrical back to the shop to close any openings behind the electrical box. He added new insulation and drywall. The Animal Control folks were also involved in the safe relocation of the furry little animals, and so far, we haven't had a repeat incident. The insurance company's investigator reviewed the findings and agreed with our report. Trish has already been reimbursed for the damage to her shop caused by the animals."

Derrick's eyes found Trish's again, and they locked their gaze for a few moments. *He looks so amazing in his uniform*, she thought, and felt the flutter of her heart turn into a pounding that filled her ears. She was lost in those big brown eyes until her trance was broken, and she listened to the rest of his speech.

"If you'll recall, the town beautification project added a dozen Red Oak Trees along Main Street several years ago. Chipmunks love these trees, so I'm surprised we haven't had more issues caused by an abundance of chipmunks in the area." Derrick chuckled. "For now, we'll call this issue closed. Any questions on this item?"

A few questions were asked and answered.

"Moving on to the 'time-expired' issue," Derrick continued. "This one is a bit more complicated. In preparation for today's meeting, I had the town clerk pull records of every ticket the automated parking system issued. Since spring, three hundred-thirty-eight tickets have been issued. With the increase in traffic during the summer months, we typically see an increase in parking tickets for time expired. Let's compare these three months against last year during the same time. Last year, we only issued ninety-eight parking tickets for time expired. We've tripled the number of tickets."

Derrick paused for a minute to let the numbers sink in and began again. "There was also a significant increase in complaints, especially from our residents, some of whom were vocal. Several merchants asked me to research the issue, but after an initial investigation, I couldn't find any irregularities with the meters."

He had to pause due to the number of complaints being shouted from the audience. "Please, calm down and let me finish. I have more to say on the topic." Derrick waited for the room to get quiet.

"In a weird chain of events, we've identified the issue. If you watch the video on the screen at the front of the room, you'll see the situation unfold."

The room got quiet as the video appeared on the screen, and Derrick explained what people were seeing. Thanks to a new police recruit with a technology background, he was able to edit hours and hours of video, along with the use of fast forward and other technologies to show the watering of the plants, the overflow dripping into the meters, and the red 'time-expired' flag popping up in the window. Derrick finished by turning over the microphone to Mark Brooks, who explained the water mixture and the report from the parking meter manufacturer, who also tested the plant-water cocktail and confirmed it was causing issues with the meters.

Derrick retook the microphone, "To sum it up, we have a problem, but thanks to Mark's creative thinking, we identified an easy solution. Looking at the hanging baskets, we noticed they are all on the north side of the poles. If the maintenance crews move the baskets to the south side of the poles, no meters would be impacted by dripping water. Hence, the problem would be solved. The crews will have the baskets moved by the end of the week and before the Labor Day festivities. Problem solved."

Mark and Derrick sat down, and the Mayor banged his gavel several times to regain order. "We want to thank Chief Williams and Mr. Brooks for their research and solving our parking meter debacle. The city will refund fines for the meters impacted by the water issue. If you don't want to stay for the remainder of the agenda items, please leave now while we take a five-minute break."

Derrick had to stay to review the Labor Day festivities, he walked over to Trish. "That went well. I'm glad we've settled two of the issues on the list, although we'll still have a few complaints about how we let the parking meter issue happen in the first place." Derrick moved closer to Trish and lightly touched her arm. He could feel the heat where their bodies connected. He moved closer to whisper in her ear. "I can't wait until this meeting is over and we find a quiet place to…" Before he could finish what he was saying, he was interrupted.

Mrs. Lester, the town busybody, called his name. "Chief Williams, I want a word with you." Derrick expected some complaint from her, which would be the norm.

"How can I help you, Mrs. Lester?"

"I want to thank you for solving the two issues. No one else could determine what was happening, yet you solved both problems. We can all get back to celebrating the upcoming Labor Day weekend. Way too much time was wasted on chit-chat about meters and alarms. If you ask me, much to do about nothing."

"Thank you for the compliment, but I didn't solve the alarm problem at Crystal Lake Gifts. Jack Burnett solved it.

I'm the messenger of good news. I'm glad we were able to stop the irritating alarms."

"Humph. You sure don't know how to take a compliment. A person can't even be nice to you. Young man, say thank you in the future, and let me walk away and get on with my evening. You young people need to learn some better manners." With those words, Mrs. Lester left the meeting room.

Derrick and Trish waited until Mrs. Lester was out of hearing range, and they both burst out in laughter. Derrick whispered, "Mrs. Lester is one tough cookie. I'm not sure anyone can fully please her, but at least she can now move on to complain and gossip about something else."

The Mayor called the meeting back to order, and those remaining in the room took their seats. The coordinator for the Labor Day events reviewed the plans, responded to questions, and turned the floor back over to the Mayor, who finished up the meeting with a reminder the Labor Day event was the biggest one of the year. He needed everyone's cooperation to make it a successful day. After a few finishing remarks, the meeting was adjourned.

Trish got swept up in the crowd and didn't get a chance to talk to Derrick, who had a line of constituents waiting to talk to him. Trish decided to leave. She was tired from the long day, yet was happy to put these two irritating issues to rest.

As she walked outside, she saw the sky had turned overcast, blocking out the moon and the stars. She wasn't sure why she suddenly felt a bit gray, and her feelings also seemed to be a bit cloudy, like the sky. She was still conflicted about her feelings for Derrick. She was getting in deeper and deeper, but was she actually in love with him? Could she forget the past and move forward? Walking away from Town Hall, she thought a good night's sleep might help clear her cloudy thoughts and the weather.

CHAPTER THIRTY

After Monday's Town Council meeting, everyone was busy preparing for the Labor Day festivities, and the next few days flew by quickly. Trish didn't have time to get together with Derrick.

Labor Day fell on a Saturday, and luckily, the weather was sunny and warm—the perfect day to celebrate outside. Trish was excited to start the day, so she got up early, had a quick cup of coffee in her room, and dressed comfortably so she was ready to enjoy the day.

Since it was a holiday, the inn was quieter than usual for six am on a Saturday. She tried not to make a sound as she left her room, descended the stairs, and peeped into the dining room. Looking inside, she didn't see anyone but noticed the room was fully equipped for breakfast to start in an hour.

Trish quickly walked down the hall to the kitchen, and as she got closer to the door, she could hear voices. Walking inside, she saw Peter and Amanda heavily engaged in preparing the breakfast buffet and working on the picnic hamper lunches several of the guests had previously ordered.

"Happy Labor Day, my friends," Trish said while doing a sloppy salute. "Are you two ready for today? I know from experience how crazy it will get."

Amanda hugged Trish, "We are as ready as possible, but we know a few last-minute fire drills will pop up. As much as we plan, it never fails that something unexpected happens. The good news is we've run the gamut of challenges over the years, so hopefully, nothing will happen that we can't handle."

From across the room, Peter commented, "Yeah, I feel as prepared as possible, but I'll also keep an open mind that something unexpected could happen. As far as the food and picnic hampers are concerned, we have those covered, so if something unexpected does happen, I'll feel better prepared to handle it quickly."

"I've got to get going since we decided to open the shop for a few hours this morning," Trish glanced at her friends all dressed in the same boatneck style shirt in deep red with blue and white embroidered designs. "I'm riding my motorcycle to make it easy to navigate the crowded streets. I'm glad we all decided to wear the matching shirts Sarah's team made for us."

Amanda added, "It will also make it easier for us to find each other in the crowd."

After Amanda gave her a quick hug, Trish walked back to the lobby to see if Cassidy was there yet so she could check with her and see how she was doing. Since she was less than two weeks away from her due date, her doctor permitted her to spend no more than two hours per day at the inn if she promised to stay off her feet as much as possible. Trish expected to see her but noticed that one of the part-timers was at the desk, and since she was engaged in a conversation with a guest, she didn't want to interrupt.

Trish went out the back entrance, pulled her motorcycle out of the underground garage, donned her bright pink helmet, and headed to town.

She was glad she left extremely early because Main Street already had a lot of extra vehicles and pedestrian traffic. She had planned to open the shop at nine o'clock, but if she were ready earlier, she'd go ahead and turn the sign to open.

An hour later, Trish turned the sign to open and unlocked the front door. A young couple entered the shop. When the woman, who looked about thirty, saw Trish's shirt, she said she loved it and asked if they sold them. It immediately hit Trish. They should have ordered some for the shop instead of the standard-themed tee shirts, but it was too late for today. She'd be sure to do so for the next holiday.

"Thank you for the compliment. These were made for us by the local artisan group, and we sell many of their handmade items in the shop, but these were made for the people helping to organize today's activities. You made me realize that we should offer similar ones for sale here, and I'll be sure to do that in the future. I can show you what we do have for sale, and I have one that I think you may like. Let me show you those, and I'll take twenty percent off anything you buy today for giving me the great idea for next year."

Sarah and several part-time workers came in around nine o'clock. The flow of foot traffic into the store was constant, and the sales were phenomenal. The time flew by, and before Trish had time for a second cup of coffee, it was noon and time to close the store, but there were so many shoppers that Trish couldn't lock the door and turn off the lights until fifteen minutes later.

"Phew!" Trish and Sarah exhaled a big breath simultaneously, and Trish added, "Let's close out the register, lock the bank bag and receipts in the safe, and head out. I'll come in early tomorrow and finish the accounting stuff."

Fifteen minutes later, Trish and Sarah headed to the park to enjoy lunch. Derrick planned to stop by for a quick bite if he could work it out. Tom and his sister, Leah, niece Ellie, and little Elijah were already there. Dr. Foster was on call at the hospital.

Trish saw Peter and Amanda, several of her part-time staff, and Amy from The Perk. They had reserved several picnic tables, and the guys had pulled them into a small semi-circle. Peter and Amanda had a large wagon filled with multiple picnic hampers, which held lunch for their group. Trish could already smell something delicious coming from the container Peter was opening.

"Hello, everyone. Happy Labor Day. I'm so glad we could all be together for lunch today." Trish smiled and looked around at her closest friends. She suddenly noticed that Cassidy and Jack were missing. Looking toward Amanda, she asked, "Where are Cassidy and Jack?"

"Jack called us earlier and said they decided to stay home for now and would join us later for the fireworks at the inn. With the heat and the crowds, Cassidy was more comfortable staying home with her feet up, enjoying the air conditioning. By the time the fireworks start, the temperatures will have dropped by at least ten degrees, and maybe she'll feel like joining us at the inn."

Trish frowned, "I'm disappointed they won't be here today, but I'm glad Cassidy is following her doctor's orders. When I saw her for Sit-n-Sip on the porch at the inn yesterday, she seemed a little flushed and tired. Again, she blamed it on the heat. Maybe they should stay home and not attend the fireworks."

"I hope everyone else joins us at the inn for the fireworks," Amanda said enthusiastically. "We love hosting the event, and the way the fireworks reflect off the lake is breathtaking. Luckily, Cassidy and Jack can also see them from their deck at the cottage."

The picnic went well, the food was delicious, and it was great having some downtime and relaxing in the park. Wanting to get to the inn to prep before the fireworks, the group helped Peter and Amanda clean up and return the leftovers to his car.

As they were making their final sweep of the area to be sure they didn't leave any trash behind, Trish noticed Peter seemed to be thinking about something. "Peter, is something wrong, you seem to be in deep thought?"

"Cassidy was the major force in moving the fireworks to the lake, and if she can't make it tonight, I'd like to pack a hamper for her and Jack and drop it off. Let's call them on our way back to the inn and make the offer. We'll miss them at the inn, but I'll feel better letting them know they are still included. How does that sound to you, Amanda, and Trish?"

Amanda walked over and gave Peter a big hug. "That is so sweet, and it's another reason why I love you."

The silence was quick and uncomfortable. That was the first time the group had heard either Amanda or Peter declare their love for each other. Since the group didn't know they were secretly married in Vegas, they had tried to keep their relationship low-key, but sometimes, it was difficult to hide their true feelings.

As soon as Amanda said the words, it was clear to Trish and the rest of the group that she realized she had made a mistake. Amanda's face turned scarlet,

She quickly looked at Peter, who looked back at their friends and said, "Okay, don't look so surprised. You must have already realized we are in love. We've not made it public yet, but we are in a committed relationship, and we hope you're happy for us."

Trish saw that Amanda seemed to be holding her breath, waiting for Peter to respond. Once he said they were in a committed relationship, everyone gathered around the couple and congratulations were shared along with hugs. Trish wasn't a bit surprised, only that it took the couple so long to make their relationship public. She was extremely happy for them.

"Hey, what's all the noise about?" Derrick yelled from several feet away. "I hope no one calls the police due to this rowdy crowd. I know I'm late, but I was finally able to take a short break before we relocate our efforts to the lake. I'm starving. Did you leave me anything to eat?"

Trish saw him glance her way, and her heart dropped. Here she was surrounded by couples who were overjoyed, sitting in the sunshine—Amanda and Peter had declared their love before everyone and would probably get married any day now. Sarah and Tom were smiling and holding hands and couldn't stop staring at each other. Cassidy and Jack weren't with them at the moment but were back at their lovely cottage, eagerly awaiting the birth of their baby. They'd all found the perfect dream life together.

And then there's me, she thought dismally. *When will I find my happily ever after?* She heard a small voice in her head reply, *Whenever you're ready to open up your heart and let Derrick in. You know you love him. Admit it. Stop being so stubborn.*

Peter interrupted her thoughts. "We already packed everything in the cars and are leaving for the inn. Since you're heading there anyway, why don't you follow us, and I will pull together a meal for you in the kitchen? We have a refrigerator full of fresh food, and it will only take me a couple of minutes."

Trish decided to lighten up and smiled at Derrick. "Or you could go through the drive-thru at the local fast-food restaurant if you prefer." She saw him grin. *Good, at least he's smiling.*

"If the meal includes a helping of Peter's fried chicken and potato salad, I'll follow you anywhere," Derrick said and winked at her. "Let's get going. This police officer needs more than donuts to get him through the rest of the day."

The group quickly got into their vehicles, but Derrick reached for Trish's arm before she got into her car. He slowly turned her around to face him, "I missed you this week. I saw you through the front window of your shop as I patrolled Main Street a couple of times, but I couldn't get up the nerve to come in and say hello. I'm not sure if you're still upset?"

Trish sighed. "I'm not sure of anything anymore."

Derrick gazed at her with his big puppy dog eyes. "Well, I'm not giving up on us, Trish Cavanaugh. I have fallen in love with you."

Trish watched Derrick slowly turn and walk to his patrol car, his shoulders drooping a bit. She was left speechless.

CHAPTER THIRTY-ONE

As promised, Peter called Jack to see if he and Cassidy planned to come to the inn and watch the fireworks from the lakeside. He wasn't surprised when Jack said they had decided to stay home and watch them from the deck of their cottage. Jack clarified that after trying to reason with Cassidy why they should stay home, her mother called and told her to stay home. In this case, Jack was happy to have a bossy mother-in-law. Peter quickly pulled together a hamper and drove it down the street to their house.

Back at the inn, it was a bit chaotic with all the guests returning to the inn and heading down the walkway to the lake, along with a crowd of folks from town, who parked along the roadway, driveway, and in the grass, and headed to the lakefront.

Trish was thankful that Amanda had hired a catering firm to help with the set-up, including stringing extra lights along the lakefront, setting up additional tables and chairs, and placing the fixing for s'mores beside the firepits down by the lake. They would also do most of the outdoor clean-up,

As the sun descended lower into the sky, the reflection on the lake was gorgeous, and Trish thought to herself that the sun and the lake always put on a beautiful show of colors. Tonight was a stunner. She never tired of the view and the sense of contentment it brought to her. After so many years of turmoil in her younger life, Trish treasured and valued her life in Lakeview. She wouldn't trade it for anything.

Once the sun finally disappeared below the horizon, the Mayor, who always kicked off the event, stood up on the small platform they built for him. He thanked the organizers and everyone in attendance for making the annual Labor Day festivities successful. With that, the fireworks company started the show on the other side of the lake (for safety purposes).

After thirty minutes of booms, oohs, and aahs, the final shimmering spirals drove up higher in the sky than the other fireworks and burst into a fantastic umbrella of colors and loud sizzling sounds until all the sparkles finally fizzled out, and the sky returned to its dark blue color. The crowd broke out in a loud round of applause and whistles, and suddenly, it was quiet except for the low hum of conversation.

It didn't take long for the crowd to leave, and within twenty minutes, the last car left the lot, except for those staying at the inn. Most of the guests had retired to their rooms. Everyone was tired after the long but fun day.

The only place left with lots of lights and activity was the kitchen. Trish, Peter, Amanda, Sarah, and Tom helped to unload boxes, load the commercial dishwasher, take out the trash, and prep for breakfast the following morning. Around eleven, the group sat down for a celebratory glass of champagne that Peter pulled from the refrigerator.

Derrick knocked on the kitchen door, and Peter let him in. Derrick grinned at those gathered in the kitchen. "Looks like I'm just in time. What are we celebrating?"

"We're celebrating another successful Labor Day event," Amanda said with a happy sigh. "The picnic went well, and the fireworks were spectacular." Amanda walked over to where Peter was standing. He put his arm around her back and pulled her closer.

"We're lucky to have such a great group of friends and to have added Tom and Derrick to our little band over the past year." Peter smiled. "Last year, we added Jack, and who knows who we will be added by this time next year. The bigger, the better. Let's toast to good friends and good times."

As Peter was finishing his toast, his phone rang. It was late in the evening for him to get a call. He looked at his phone and saw that it was Jack.

Peter's phone was on speaker, so everyone heard the caller loud and clear. "Don't say anything until I explain what's happening. Cassidy is in labor, and we headed to the hospital about an hour ago, luckily, right before the fireworks were over. Cassidy was at seven centimeters, so the doctor said we'd still have an hour or two before we'd be ready to move into the delivery room.

"She's doing fine, and her mother is with her, but she wants to see Trish and Amanda before she goes to the delivery room. It seems they made a pact to share this special moment. We assumed Derrick was with you, so maybe he could get the girls here quickly, and you guys could follow in your cars if you wanted to join us. I've got to run. Please get the girls here quickly, or I'll be in trouble for not making the call sooner."

Peter looked across the room at Derrick, "How fast can you get to the hospital? Cassidy is in labor and wants to see Amanda and Trish, if possible before the baby is born…"

"We heard!" the group said in unison.

The screaming and squealing from the women in the room were deafening. Trish and Amanda were grabbing shoes and purses and running out the door before Derrick could even say yes, he would happily give them a ride.

With lights flashing and sirens blaring, Derrick took the girls to the hospital in less than ten minutes. Of course, the streets were empty at this time of night, so the trip was quick. As soon as the car stopped at the emergency entrance, Trish and Amanda jumped out, yelling thank you to Derrick as they ran inside through the revolving doors.

They ran straight to the information desk, asked for Cassidy's room, and were told she was on the fourth floor in Labor and Delivery. As they started running toward the elevator, an older woman in a nurse's uniform stepped in front of them and told them to stop running. Someone could get hurt, and the ER was already full tonight.

When the elevator doors opened, they saw Cassidy's mother, Kate, waiting for them. "I'll show you the room. Only one visitor is allowed at a time besides the father, but Cassidy insisted and argued with the doctor until he agreed that both of you could visit with her, but only for five minutes. Both Jack and I agreed that you would honor his orders. Do I have your word?"

Amanda and Trish said yes simultaneously and followed Kate to a room on the other side of a semi-circular nurses' station.

It took Trish a minute for her eyes to adjust after the hallway's bright overhead lights and the room's dimmer ones. Jack was standing near the head of the bed, and Cassidy was propped up with several pillows behind her head. She had an IV drip, and her hair was pulled back from her face. She looked better than Trish had expected.

Jack moved to the foot of the bed and motioned for Trish to stand on one side and Amanda on the other. They both took one look at their friend, who was like a sister to them, and they started to cry.

Cassidy grabbed both of their hands. "Why are you crying? I'm doing fine. I'll be so happy to see our baby girl. I hope she has Jack's baby-blue eyes and dark wavy hair and…"

Before she could finish her statement, she had a contraction and started to do the breathing she had learned in class a few months earlier. Once the contraction was over, Cassidy took a few additional deep breaths and asked Jack for a few small pieces of crushed ice from the cup on her tray.

"Are you okay?" asked Trish. "That seemed to be extremely painful." Trish hated to see her friend in so much pain. She hoped the delivery would be over soon. She felt tears forming in her eyes, but she wiped them away and put a smile on her face.

"The contractions are getting worse, but that also means I'm getting closer to delivery. Before I have another contraction or the doctor kicks you out, I want to be sure we follow through with the pinky swear promise we made years ago."

Jack looked at Cassidy, then stepped out of the room for a second.

"We committed to being sisters by choice and swore that we would be with each other for all the important events in our lives." Cassidy brushed away a tear. "This is my third big event, and I couldn't do it without you. You were there when I opened the inn, you were attendants at my wedding, and now you're here when our sweet little girl comes into this world. I love you so much."

Cassidy reached into the nightstand drawer and pulled out two beautifully wrapped packages. "Open your packages. I hope you like it."

Trish and Amanda unwrapped the packages and then opened the velvet boxes. Each box held a beautiful locket with their birthstone on the front. Tears flowed down both women's cheeks.

"Open the lockets," Cassidy said excitedly.

The left side of the locket displayed a picture of the three friends, all dressed up at the Lakeview Hospital Gala two years ago. The right side was empty.

"Once our little one is old enough for a professional photograph, I'll have one made for each of you, small enough to fit on the right side of the locket, because Godmothers should always have pictures of their Goddaughters, right?"

"Godmothers? Us? You want us to both be Godmothers to your daughter?" Trish said because Amanda was crying too hard to speak.

Jack walked in and softly said, "Yes. We talked it over, and there wasn't anyone else even in the running for the job. We know that the two of you will always have her best interest at heart, and if, God forbid, anything ever happened to us, you'll help Kate raise her. How do you feel about that? I haven't heard anyone say yes yet."

Forgetting they should keep their voices down, they both yelled, YES! YES! YES!"

Another contraction hit Cassidy, and this one was a doozie. It lasted longer than the last one, and Jack could tell she was in extreme pain.

The nurse returned to the room and reminded the visitors to keep their voices down and that it was time to say their goodbyes.

After more tears and hugs, Amanda and Trish left the room and returned to the hallway, where Kate asked to see their lockets. As they opened the box to show them to Kate, she pulled an identical locket from her pocket, and as if the floodgates had opened, all three women started crying and hugging.

The nurse entered the hallway and directed the visitors to the waiting room. Kate returned to Cassidy's room, where she and Jack planned to stay with Cassidy throughout the delivery.

Two minutes later, they saw the doctor going into Cassidy's room. There was a flurry of activity, and she was wheeled off to Delivery. As the attendants rolled the hospital bed out of the room, Jack quickly yelled to his friends that it was time and that he would call them when he had an update.

And suddenly, time started to stand still. Minutes ticked off the clock like something sticky was holding back the hands. Thirty minutes went by, then forty minutes, and still no news.

Trish heard the elevator doors open, and she saw Dr. Foster walk out and head in their direction.

"Hello, everyone. I guess you're wondering what's happening in Cassidy's delivery room. Unfortunately, progress slowed down a bit, and her doctor called me in to be on standby in case a C-section was needed. After an examination, we don't think that will be necessary. Before I left the room, she was already starting to move a bit faster in the right direction." Dr. Foster briefly paused and took a long swig of the cold bottle of water a nurse had brought to him.

"Jack didn't want you to worry needlessly, so I offered to stop by to update you. I'll be here in case anything changes, but I don't think you should worry. Cassidy is a strong and determined mother-to-be, and she's decided that she wants the baby to be born before midnight. She only has fifteen minutes until then, so I'm not sure even Cassidy can make her deadline happen. Jack wasn't worried about the time the baby would be born. He was more worried about the extra stress Cassidy was putting on herself. I'll be at the nurses' station working on patient charts. I'll let you know if I hear anything."

Trish looked around the room and saw a sea of worried faces. Cassidy had never contemplated a C-Section, but it wasn't her call. Sometimes, Mother Nature had other plans. The group sat back down and tried not to look worried.

The waiting room was quiet. Everyone was waiting for the next update. Ten minutes later, the quiet was interrupted by a phone ringing, and they saw Dr. Foster pull his cell phone from his pocket, "Yes, that is good news. I'll let Jack call them. I'm heading out for the night, but don't hesitate to call me if you need me."

Before Trish could even get out of her chair to speak with Dr. Foster, Peter's phone rang, and it was Jack. It was midnight.

Jack asked Peter to put the call on speaker. "We have our perfect baby girl! She weighs seven pounds and five ounces. Mother and baby are fine. Cassidy was determined she'd be born on Labor Day, and she made it with four minutes to spare and was born at eleven-fifty-six pm. Cassidy asks that you all go home for the night. Everyone needs to get some rest. You can come back tomorrow to see us. Kate used her pull and got special approval for you to visit tomorrow at ten o'clock so you can return to the inn for Sunday brunch, but you have to promise to stay for only fifteen minutes. Cassidy sends her love. I've got to go. Hugs to all."

There was another round of tears, hugs, and congratulations.

Everyone was exhausted, so Derrick spoke up, "What a day. I think we all need to head home and get some rest. I'm happy to drive Trish back to the inn. Does anyone else need a ride?"

Peter spoke up, "We're headed to the inn. We can take Trish with us."

"If you don't mind, I'd like to take her home. We have some catching up to do. Trish, are you okay going with me?"

"Yes." That was all she could get out, since her heart was thudding in her ears again.

Tom was taking Sarah home, so they headed out with Peter and Amanda close behind them.

As Derrick helped Trish into the car, he whispered, "Once we get to the inn, do you mind if we take a quick walk down to the lake? I guess I don't want this night to end."

Trish briefly paused. Was she ready to be alone with Derrick, especially when her emotions were so raw? She surprised herself when she replied, "That sounds perfect."

CHAPTER THIRTY-TWO

They were quiet on their ride to the inn. Both seemed lost in their own thoughts. Trish stole a glance at Derrick's silhouette. He really was handsome, but looking at him evoked other feelings, and those darn goosebumps started to run down her arms. What else was she feeling? She couldn't put her finger on it. And then, she realized she also felt safe and loved. Loved by Derrick! *What's happening to me?*

And just like that, there was clarity. Trish realized that she loved Derrick. Maybe it was hard to identify the feeling at first since she'd never truly been in love beyond the puppy love she shared with Derrick when they were teenagers. She never saw true love between her parents either, but she had seen true love between Cassidy and Jack, and she had all the same emotions and feelings Cassidy talked about.

As they pulled into a parking spot and Derrick put the car in park, Trish waffled about admitting her feelings. *Was this the right time? Should I wait to profess my love? Am I truly in love?*

Before Trish could decide what to do, Derrick had already jumped out of the car and opened her door, waiting for her to get out.

"Are you getting out of the car, or did you change your mind about walking around the lake?"

Trish looked up at Derrick and seemed to be surprised they were already at the lake and parked. She looked at him and smiled as she got out of the car. "Let's go sit on the bench at the edge of the lake." The area was well lit and they could see the moon shimmering on the lake. It was a gorgeous evening, yet it was late, and the area was quiet.

Once they were settled, Derrick started to say something, but Trish placed her hand on his arm and quietly said, "Let me go first. I have something I need to say."

Trish turned toward him so she could look into those dark brown eyes. "Derrick, I've been a fool. The terrible relationship my parents had and some disastrous short-term boyfriends I've had over the years made me leery of romance. I thought all I needed was a successful business, and my good friends and life would be perfect.

"Maybe it was to a certain point, but you reentered my life and turned it upside down. I started to feel the gap of not having love in my life. You made me feel things I hadn't felt before, and my heart started to open up. And, when I was sure I was falling for you, I learned you had secrets you hadn't shared. The thing that hurt the most was that you didn't trust me enough to share that part of your life with me."

Trish paused to catch her breath and Derrick again started to say something, but she placed her pointer finger across his lips in a sign for him to remain quiet.

"I need to finish what I want to say, or I might chicken out. When I saw the love between Cassidy and Jack tonight as they waited for the birth of their daughter, it hit me like a ton of bricks. I wanted what they had. I want it all. The love, the marriage, the children, and the cottage with the white picket fence. And most importantly, I want it with you."

Trish didn't wait to take a breath or to pause. "I'm in love with you, Derrick Williams. Totally and hopelessly in love. Can you forgive me for doubting your love and taking so long to admit my feelings?"

Derrick didn't respond with words. Instead, he quickly stood up, pulled Trish to her feet, and pulled her into a passionate embrace and kiss. The kiss wasn't playful or sweet. It was full of passion and love. The kiss went on until Trish pulled back.

"I guess that means you love me and forgive me for wasting time? When I think of all the times I could have been in your arms, I'm mad at myself."

"Maybe this will help you forgive yourself because I sure have." Pulling her into his arms again, Derrick kissed her lips, then moved to nibble on her ear before returning to her lips one more time.

"Did you enjoy the kisses?"

"Um. That was nice," Trish said in a playful way.

"Again, what's with the nice description? Is that all? I guess I'll have to do better." Derrick pulled her closer to his body and claimed her lips. Trish could feel his warm body against hers. She heard the soft swishing sound of water hitting the dock, and she could hear an owl off in the distance, but most of all, she could hear her heart beating. She wondered if Derrick could hear it too. But, once he parted her lips and dove deeper, Trish couldn't think of anything else. Her emotions and body were focused on the passionate kiss that created heat and made her heart race. "I take it back. It wasn't just nice, it was perfect."

When Derrick released her lips and sightly stepped back, Trish felt a rush of cool air between them. She wanted to reduce the space between them, but she could tell Derrick was reaching for something in his pocket.

"Derrick, are you reaching for your police radio? Please don't answer it. Give us a few more minutes together."

Before she realized what was happening, Derrick was down on one knee, opening a small velvet box. "Trish, I love you so deeply. I never thought I would feel this way. I've been in love with you since I first responded to the alarm at your store on the day you planned to open your shop. You looked so upset. I wanted to put my arms around you and protect you. My heart immediately remembered how it felt in high school all those years ago, and I fell hard and fast. I tried to take it slow, but I couldn't.

"I want us to be partners. I respect how hard you've worked to get your business to the level of success it's at today, and I will never get in the way of your time with your friends. But, at the end of the day, I want you home at night in our bed to make passionate love and create a future together. Will you marry me?"

Trish looked in stunned silence at the gorgeous marquis-shaped diamond on a gold band shining against blue velvet. "You had me at I love you deeply. Yes, I'll marry you. I can't wait to be your wife. I also want us to be life partners, supporting what matters the most to each other. I know you'll always be there for me, protect me, and be the husband I've always dreamed of."

After the festivities earlier in the day—the fireworks, Cassidy's delivery, and now the engagement—Trish and Derrick were both on emotional overload, which turned into a desperate need for sleep.

Derrick walked Trish to the inn's door. "I love you. You've made me so happy. Get a good night's sleep. I'll be by tomorrow to take you to the hospital to see Cassidy and the baby."

A surprised look crossed Trish's face, "I realized I don't even know the name of Cassidy and Jack's baby. They had wanted to keep it a secret until she was born, but with all the chaos, we didn't get the chance to ask. Leave it to Cassidy's best friends to overlook important details like the baby's name."

"You'll find out soon enough. Get some sleep. I'll be here at nine-forty-five to drive you to the hospital."

Trish walked inside, closed and locked the door, and dreamily headed to her room. Once she got ready for bed, she sat in the chair by the window that looked out over the lake. She thanked God for her good friends, good fortune with her business, and the love of a good man. If you'd asked her ten years ago what her life would be like today, it certainly wouldn't have been this bright. She said a quick prayer for good health for Cassidy, Jack, and the new baby, and slipped into bed. She was so tired her eyes closed immediately when her head hit the pillow.

CHAPTER THIRTY-THREE

Even after not getting to bed until early morning, Peter, Amanda, and Trish were up early and in the kitchen. They wanted to get everything ready so they could visit Cassidy and see the new baby at the hospital at ten o'clock.

It was decided Amanda and Trish would ride with Derrick, and Peter would stay at the inn to work with the staff to prepare everything for the brunch, which started at eleven o'clock. It would be a scramble to get it all done, but Peter didn't want to let Cassidy down, so he worked like a crazy chef to get everything done on time.

"I need to go to my room, change my clothes, and grab my purse," Trish said as she finished stacking various sizes of dishes on a cart to wheel into the dining room.

Amanda looked up from rolling silverware into crisp white napkins, "While you do that, I'll pack the lunch Peter made for Cassidy and Jack in one of those 'stay warm' bags we have in the storage room. I told him to do something simple like sandwiches, but nope, not our Peter. He insisted we take quiche, sliced maple ham, fluffy buttered potatoes, and a small salad. And, of course, he included brownies and cookies. I'm not sure Cassidy will be ready to eat a full meal, but I'm sure Jack hasn't had a decent meal in two days."

Right on time, Derrick pulled up to the back entrance of the inn and walked into the kitchen. "Everyone ready to go? We don't want to be late."

Trish walked over to Derrick, gave him a brief hug, and pushed him back out the kitchen door and down the steps to the parking lot.

"What's wrong?" Derrick asked.

"I don't want you to get the wrong idea. I'm gloriously happy to be engaged, but today is Cassidy and Jack's day. I put my gorgeous ring on a chain around my neck and slid it under my sweater. Are you okay with waiting to share our news with our friends?"

"You're so considerate of your friends. It's another reason I love you so much," Derrick pulled Trish into his arms, leaned down, and kissed her.

"Hey, you two. We'll never get to see the baby or find out her name if you don't stop all that mushy stuff. Let's go." Amanda walked over to Derrick's car, got in the back seat, and closed the door.

Ten minutes later, the trio walked into Cassidy's room. Jack was sitting in a chair beside her bed, and Cassidy held the sleeping baby. Cassidy put her finger to her lips in a gesture to say don't be as loud as you typically are…let the baby sleep.

Hugs were exchanged, tears flowed, and Jack said, "I smell something delicious, and I'm starving. Did Peter send me a goody bag?"

"Yes, he did. Peter sent enough to feed everyone on this floor," Amanda said as she laid out red, white, and blue napkins on the table, placed paper plates and utensils on the side, and opened the containers. "Everything is ready, so help yourself."

Cassidy looked at the food and smiled. "Would one of you like to hold our little angel so I can eat? I've been cleared for a regular meal. Maybe they meant a typical hospital meal, but this is way better. Please thank Peter for us."

Trish was the first to walk over and reach for the baby, but she suddenly stopped, looked at Cassidy, and said, "Wait a minute. We realized after we left the hospital last night, we don't know what you decided to name her. What is our Goddaughter's name?"

Cassidy looked down at the sweet bundle of joy in her arms, "Please meet Katherine Kristine Burnett. Katherine after my mother. Kristine after Jack's mother. We plan to call her Katie. My mother was never called Katie, so there shouldn't be any confusion. What do you think of her name?"

When Cassidy looked up at her friends, tears rolled down their faces. "If you two start crying, it will make me cry, and I've already cried tears of joy all morning."

Trish carefully took Katie from Cassidy and walked her over so Amanda and Derrick could get a good look. Katie was adorable. She had Jack's big blue eyes, and the little bit of hair she had looked blond, but of course, eye and hair color might change over time.

Derrick stepped back and let Trish enjoy the baby, but something caught in his throat when he took another look at her holding the little pink bundle of joy. He said a silent prayer that one day, his son or daughter would be in her arms.

A few minutes later, a nurse came into the room and shooed them all out. Since they knew the special visiting time was a favor to Kate, they left without protest but said they would return for the evening visiting hour.

Before Cassidy and Jack brought Katie home the next day, Trish had arranged for Peter, Amanda, and Sarah to join her at the little cottage by the lake. They cleaned the entire house so every surface shone brightly, and all the laundry was washed, folded, and put away. Peter had prepared several meals that only needed reheating and placed them in the refrigerator along with the other perishable items they had purchased at the grocery store on their way to Cassidy's house. Finally, Trish filled the cookie jar with fresh chocolate chip cookies, which happened to be Cassidy's favorite, and left a bowl of fresh fruit on the kitchen island.

The last thing on their list was to place a rocking chair by the window in the nursery. The rocker originally belonged to Cassidy's grandmother, known as Grams. It needed some repairs and had been in the inn's attic for several years. Cassidy had intended to get it repaired and refinished, but she never did. Jack remembered Cassidy had wanted to get the rocker refurbished and had asked Sarah to find the perfect carpenter for the job.

Once it was done, it was perfect. Trish placed it in the nursery, near the window overlooking the lake. It was a sentimental piece for Cassidy, and Jack wanted her to feel like her Grams was there to watch over little Katie.

With the rocking chair in place, the group looked around and smiled. They were tired but happy. Thanks to their friends, Cassidy, Jack, and Katie would enter a warm and welcoming home later that day.

After dinner that evening at the inn, the friends walked to the lake to watch the gorgeous evening sky. It was perfect weather for early September. They knew these warm evenings were short in number since fall started earlier in Maine than in most of the country.

Sarah and Tom, Peter and Amanda, and Trish and Derrick stood together—three couples united by the inn, the lake, and Cassidy. The couples held hands and spoke about the events of the past few days, which turned into a walk down memory lane.

Trish looked at Peter and Amanda, who were so obliviously in love, and wondered when they'd announce their engagement. Then her gaze moved to Sarah and Tom, who seemed to be taking their relationship slowly.

Derrick couldn't suppress a big yawn, "I hate to break up this wonderful evening, but I have the early shift in the morning and need to get some sleep. Trish, I'll walk you back to the inn."

Peter added, "We all need a good night's sleep."

The group walked back up to the bottom of the stairs leading to the inn's front door. Trish reached out to hug Amanda, and the chain that held her engagement ring slid out of her sweater.

"Trish, what's hanging from your chain? I've seen you wear the chain before, but it never had something shiny hanging from it. OMG! Is that a ring? Are you and Derrick engaged?"

Trish looked at Derrick, and he nodded his head up and down to signify it was time to come clean with their friends. "Yes. We're engaged. It happened after Cassidy had her baby two nights ago, but we didn't want to take anything away from their special time, so we decided to wait until we were all together to share our news, but I guess the secret is out."

Derrick pulled Trish into a hug, but Sarah and Amanda pushed him aside so they could hug her. The sound level was elevated as the girls giggled and talked over each other.

"That is so exciting!" Amanda beamed. "We'll keep it quiet until you can tell Cassidy yourself tomorrow. She'll be so happy for you. I'm so happy for you two. WOW! Another wedding at the inn. I assume you'll want to get married at the inn?"

"Yes, Amanda, we want to get married at the inn." Trish said. "There is no date yet, but we think a Spring wedding would be nice, and it leaves plenty of time to plan without me becoming a bridezilla."

Peter walked over to shake hands with Derrick, "Congratulations. I think of Trish as a sister, so this is your only warning. If you hurt her, Jack and I will hurt you. Of course, I'm not sure how we'll do that since you're in much better physical shape than we are, but heed our warning."

Derrick laughed. "I will absolutely heed your warning. I promise to take excellent care of Trish and never hurt her. I hope you and Jack will be my best men. You've become like brothers to me, so having you both stand up for me feels right. What do you think?"

A smile broke out on Peter's face, "Of course. I'd be honored. Now, can you help me get these women moving so we can all get some sleep tonight? I'm beat."

The group said their final goodnights and congratulations and headed to their homes. It had been an event-filled couple of days, and it was clear from the yawning everyone was eager to get home.

A short time later, Trish got ready for bed and sat by the window overlooking the lake. She had so much to be grateful for, and tonight, when she said her prayers, she remembered to add little Katie.

Without any siblings and both her parents gone, she knew what it was like to be alone in the world. That all changed when she met Cassidy. Trish knew she had found her best friend, and then along came Amanda. Years later, their little group expanded to include Peter, Sarah, Tom, Jack, and Derrick. Of course, Cassidy's family always treated her like one of their own, for which she was so thankful. Now, marrying Derrick, she realized she was creating her own family.

Thinking about little Katie, she also felt her biological clock ticking. Derrick had said he wanted to have children with her, and she wanted the same thing. Being more traditional, she wanted the wedding first and then the children. Which reminded her that she needed to get moving on planning if she wanted a Spring wedding.

Trish turned off the lights and slipped into bed. She kept the window slightly open, but with the fall approaching, the room was chilly. She reached down to the foot of the bed and pulled up the light quilt she kept there. It was her favorite one since Nana had given it to her.

She hoped her Nana could see her and was proud of the journey she'd forged and the woman she'd become. She blew a kiss toward the ceiling in a gesture of sending a kiss to her grandmother in heaven.

As she drifted off to sleep, she could hear the water from the lake slightly hitting the dock, and off in the distance, she heard an owl hooting. When she was younger, she always thought the wise old owl was saying, 'Who?' and took that to mean who she'd marry. Years later, she knew the answer to that question…it was Derrick.

She, Cassidy, Amanda, and Sarah—four female friends who had each experienced heartbreak and loss but hadn't totally locked their hearts away from love—realized how they had overcome their challenges and now had love filling their hearts instead of heartbreak. She couldn't wait to marry Derrick and see what the future held for their little group of friends.

With that, she took a deep, cleansing breath, closed her eyes, and drifted off to sleep.

EPILOGUE

It was a gorgeous early November day at Crystal Lake Inn. It was unusually warm for a Fall day in Maine, but good fortune had provided a string of warm, sunny days. By contrast, the vibrant fall foliage was stunning. The leaves had changed colors and looked like an artist's palette with every shade of red, orange, and gold. The lake reflected these colors and added light blue and white from the few puffy clouds in the otherwise bright blue sky.

A small group of about twenty-five assembled in the large dining room at the inn for a special occasion. Cassidy and Jack stood in the front of the room, one on either side of their local clergyman. Little Katie was snug in Godmother Amanda's arms and slept despite the activity around her. Trish, her other Godmother, was standing right beside her.

Today was Katie's six-week-old birthday. It was a little earlier than the Burnett family usually would have held a Christening, but Jack was leaving for an extended book tour in a few days. After some debate, Cassidy and Jack moved their little family to his New York City condominium and made that their home during the year-long tour. Of course, not everyone was thrilled with them moving away, even if it was only for a year, but resolved they could always visit frequently.

Cassidy's mother, Kate, and her husband, Duncan Moore, stood proudly on the other side of Cassidy and Jack. Trish noticed that Kate kept dabbing her eyes with an embroidered hanky. She recalled Cassidy telling her that Grams gave it to Kate when Cassidy was christened. It seemed perfect for the event, and it was getting put to good use.

Derrick and Peter stood slightly behind Trish and Amanda. Both women gently placed a kiss on Katie's forehead and handed her over to the proud parents. A slight baby bump under Amanda's gorgeous navy blue dress was barely noticeable as she turned sideways to stand next to Peter. It seemed there was another new secret waiting to be revealed.

Trish's mind wandered briefly as she looked at Peter and Amanda. She recalled the dinner a few weeks ago when the couple came clean on their elopement in Vegas. Everyone was thrilled and yet a bit disappointed they hadn't gotten to share in the special day, but they understood Amanda treasured her quiet life in Lakeview. An elopement was the only way to prevent her influential business family from pressuring her into a big wedding.

Peter had shared with Trish that, for similar reasons, he hadn't accepted Coco Diamond's offer to be the head chef at her new upscale restaurant in New York City. Amanda had previously lived in the fast lane of the rich and famous, and when she'd had enough, she ran to Lakeview and the inn. She never looked back.

Accepting the role with Coco would have pushed them back into the limelight. After weighing the pros and cons, they quietly decided to stay in Lakeview.

Trish looked around the room. She could feel the love and promises of things to come radiating from those she held so dear.

Glancing over at little Katie, Trish was surprised the baby continued to be quiet and content. She seemed to know something special was happening, and she was the center of attention, especially as she was dressed in an elegant designer outfit with hand-smocking and matching blanket. An outrageously expensive gift from Aunt Amanda from one of her designer friends in Paris.

Trish was so happy Sarah and Tom had joined them. She noticed that Sarah was smiling, yet she also noticed a few tears trickled down her cheek. These two continued to take it slow, but their love seemed to blossom daily. Sarah had shared with Trish that she was hoping for a special Christmas gift this year.

After the ceremony, as usual for this group, they ate. Peter had cooked a fantastic meal, similar to his famous Sunday Brunch and everyone ate way too much.

The group visited and reminisced about the past year and amazing events including the expansion of Crystal Lake Gifts, most of them overcoming past challenges and finding love, and the birth of Katie.

By late afternoon, Katie was no longer that quiet and angelic baby of earlier in the day. Her parents knew it was time to take her home, feed her, and get her down for a long overdue nap. They said their goodbyes, and since they were leaving for New York the following morning, there were extra hugs and more tears.

After walking the Burnetts to their car, Trish and Derrick decided to walk around the lake. With the sun setting earlier every day, Trish knew to grab her coat and gloves before they left the inn.

Sitting on a bench by the lake, Derrick pulled Trish closer and brought up the subject of their wedding plans. "I know you're in full planning mode for the wedding, but after today, I also wanted to bring up a delicate subject. How do you feel about having children soon after we are married? With every birthday, I feel time slipping away, and I want a house full of children. Is that okay with you, or would you rather wait?"

Trish looked into Derrick's eyes, "There's a lot of moving parts to figure out. Who will run the shop? Where will we live? Will I be able to get pregnant right away? We need to resolve so many questions before I can fully commit…but I feel the same way you do."

Trish took Derrick's hand in hers, "I had something to prove to others and, maybe most importantly, to myself. Being the premier anchor store on Main Street has been a dream come true. Sales are beyond anything I ever imagined. I can't walk away from all of that. I guess I can't fully put my past behind me. At least not yet."

Derrick spoke quietly, "I fully support your business ventures. I know how hard you worked to overcome your past. Even if you don't feel you've achieved everything you promised your Nana, if you're honest with yourself, you'll realize you've already accomplished more than you ever imagined. It's time to accept you're one driven and formidable businesswoman."

Derrick paused, pulled Trish closer, and continued, "On the other two points, you seem happy in my house. I was thrilled when you agreed to move in with me last month. Why don't we continue to live in my house while we look for something bigger to hold that brood of children we plan to have? And, on the last point, I'm happy to consider adoption if we don't have biological children. I always see needy children in my line of work, and bringing one into our family would warm my heart. Questions answered and problems solved."

"It seems you have our future perfectly mapped out, and I'm happy to ride that trail with you, but right now, I'm freezing, so let's walk back to your car and turn the heat up." Trish briskly rubbed her gloved hands together.

Derrick smiled and pulled Trish closer to him on the bench. "Speaking of children, maybe we should hurry home and get started. That's the best way to quickly warm up." He pulled Trish closer for a deeper hug and a passionate kiss.

Derrick released her from the hug, stood up, and pulled Trish off the bench. When she stood up, they were startled when they heard something crack under their feet. Afraid of what they had stepped on, they looked down and immediately burst out laughing.

Once they caught their breath, Derrick reached for Trish's hand again, and they continued walking to their car to go home.

After taking a few steps, Trish stopped, turned around, and started laughing again. She couldn't believe they had stepped on a pile of acorns. "I guess it's a sign we should name our firstborn Little Acorn."

And with that, the couple left the lake, got in their car, and took one last look at the stunning view.

Crystal Lake presented them with a full view of the setting sun, a parting gift as they drove away, Trish thought to herself, *we are literally driving off into the sunset. Life doesn't get any better than this.*

THE END

TO MY READERS

Readers are the backbone of the publishing industry. We wouldn't have authors or the publishing industry without you. Readers make this industry one of the most powerful in the world.

Specifically, I want to thank my readers. You have become the most rewarding part of being an author. I read every review and social media post, and your insights and suggestions stick in my mind as I write. In this book, there are subtle references or scenes prompted by readers. I hope you find the one you recommended.

Crystal Lake Gifts is book two in the Crystal Lake Series. I'm working towards publishing a third book in the series. If you enjoyed this book, please take a minute to leave a review. You can easily do it using one of the links below.

My books are available at Amazon and most online retailers. Visit my website for additional information and links to order my other books.

www.amazon.com/s?k=crystal+lake+inn+by+susan+w+green%2F
www.facebook.com/booksbysusanwgreen
www.booksbysusanwgreen.com

Connect with us:

ABOUT THE AUTHOR

Susan W. Green, an award-winning author, writes lighthearted romance novels with female leads and sprinkles interesting challenges and humor throughout her books. ***CRYSTAL LAKE GIFTS*** is her second novel in the Crystal Lake Series, each of which can be read as a stand-alone book. Her debut novel, ***Crystal Lake Inn***, won an Independent Press Award and was distributed in eight countries.

Retired from a 35-year executive banking career, when she's not writing, you'll find her partnering with universities and women's organizations, serving on boards, helping entrepreneurs, mentoring, and reading. She's also a coffee lover, so you can expect to find coffee mentioned in all her books.

Susan and her husband reside in Fair Hill, MD, where they enjoy peaceful surroundings, hosting family and friends…and sitting on the front porch with a good cup of coffee.